Also by Geraldine Birch

The Swastika Tattoo

Vision of a Happy Life
A Memoir

SEDONA

CITY OF REFUGEES

GERALDINE BIRCH

ISBN: 978-0-578-56572-9

Published by Birch Treehouse Publishing

2019 – Third Edition

TABLE OF CONTENTS

CHAPTER 1

Kathleen Sullivan Buckley set her jaw and her hat against a cold north wind as she walked toward her husband's funeral.

God forgive me, she thought. Even hell is too good for the bastard.

Suddenly feeling naked against the gale and her own raw feelings, she stopped for a moment to gather herself together, took a deep breath, and felt the sting of unrepentant hatred flood her soul.

Preoccupied with her sinful thoughts, Kathleen failed to keep up with her mother, Rose, who walked ahead and stopped suddenly at the steps leading up to the church. The older woman looked frail. One small, knurled hand ravaged by arthritis gripped a rosary, while the other gathered her cloth coat about her throat in an effort to keep out the gnawing April wind.

Scott Buckley's expensive bronze casket was being carried past the rustic Stations of the Cross that stood outside the adobe-styled church, and when Kathleen caught up with her mother the sight of the casket momentarily jarred her.

Rose pulled a handkerchief out of her coat pocket and dabbled at her eyes. She looked apprehensively over at her daughter. "I'm sorry, Kathleen—sorry for it all."

Kathleen nodded but did not answer. Instead, she felt a sudden, sharp pain in her left clavicle where Scott had broken it. Automatically, she reached up to rub it and reflected on her mother's remark, which flung a long, dark shadow back through her years with Scott—years that had moved her into middle age and stripped her of her faith in the Roman Catholic Church.

Kathleen turned away from the casket, trying to hide the malice in her eyes and for a moment she took in the breathtaking red rock scenery of Sedona. Here it was, just a few days past Easter, and the vermilion buttes were still dressed in a mantle of white, accenting the redness of the rocks. The recent spring snow storm had descended upon the tourist community as suddenly as Pentecost.

The scene before her was like stepping back in time two thousand years. Three life-size crosses representing the crucifixion stood across the parking lot from St. John Vianney Catholic Church, acting as a backdrop to the open vista of imposing buttes. The stark landscape spread as far north toward Oak Creek Canyon as the eye could see, somehow reminding Kathleen of the Holy Land, although she never knew why. She had lived in the northern Arizona community for more than a decade and never ceased to be amazed at its striking scenery. Taking in the view, Kathleen involuntarily shrugged her shoulders as if to shake off her attachment to the place. Her six months away from Sedona only made her realize the red rock monoliths were both its blessing and its curse, and perhaps her own. She may have left Sedona to save herself, but the splendor of the place was burned into her being.

As Kathleen turned back to view the casket, the wind whipped her dark hair loose from the bun at the nape of her neck, giving her a slightly disheveled appearance. Rose reached up to her daughter and gently, lovingly tucked the unruly hair behind Kathleen's ear.

"There," the older woman said. "You need to appear the best you can today."

The daughter did not respond, but the vacant look in her dark brown eyes prompted Rose to heave a heavy sigh.

Kathleen's cousin, Charley, came up beside her and put his arm around her shoulder. A thin, angular man, Charley was five years older than Kathleen, but his gray hair and full, bushy beard made him appear older than fifty.

She leaned into him, feeling sickened by the cross of loathing she carried for her husband. She eyed the gleaming bronze coffin with unease. Its ornamentation was overdone, just as was everything Scott owned. Simplicity was not a trait of Scott Buckley, even in death. She realized that inside the coffin lay the remains of the man she had been married to for years, his body smashed beyond recognition, his immortal soul released into God's care, and she was glad for it, glad that she no longer had to feel the pain of his physical presence.

Kathleen left Scott six months before his death because of his addictions. He loved his fine whiskey and his assorted women, most of them lonely seekers who came to Sedona looking for spiritual enlightenment from high-priced New Age gurus.

And Scott knew where to find them, often corralled at some hotel bar murmuring about the spiritual wonders they had experienced in Sedona that day and charmed them easily into his finely-spun web of lies and deceit. A superb dinner at one of Sedona's high-priced restaurants, a bit of close dancing, and the lonesome women fell easily into bed with him hoping this would be more than just a one-night stand. And, often it was, until Scott grew tired of the New Age babble they spouted with enthusiasm, believing everything in their lives were related to the crystals they hung around their necks.

Kathleen's Irish-Catholic stoic temperament carried her through most of her trials with Scott, his belligerent language and behavior toward her, never seen in public. However, it was his last volatile attack that finally forced her to face the state of her empty marriage.

That day was crushed into her consciousness.

Business at Buckley Hardware—often the gathering place for local merchants to meet over a steaming cup of coffee—had grown stagnant with the opening in town of a large discount hardware chain, threatening the base of Scott's power within the community. It never mattered to Scott that he and his brother, Philip, owned ten other hardware stores throughout the state. For Scott, the Sedona store was his baby, his personal pride.

On that day, Scott called Kathleen at home, something he rarely did. She heard an edge to his voice and asked if something was wrong. Besides a sagging month-end financial report on the Sedona store, Scott told Kathleen he had spent a frustrating hour on the phone with the U.S. Forest Service District Ranger.

"This land trade with the Forest Service is getting on my nerves. Now I'm told the property has to go through some kind of search for archeological artifacts. Frankly, I don't give a good goddamn that a stinking Indian decided to bury his relatives on my land 500 years ago!"

When Kathleen put the phone down, she had a vague sense of uneasiness, but the feeling passed as she worked through the day, trying to finish a free-lance writing assignment for *Arizona Highways*. She didn't hear Scott as he entered the house that evening and was unaware of him as he stood silently watching her from the doorway of her office, anger clouding his dark features as he gulped from a Jack Daniel's bottle that he'd grabbed a moment earlier from the bar.

"That's all you do, you bitch, work at that goddamn computer!"

Kathleen jumped at the sound of his voice and instantly got up from her desk.

"Scott! I'm sorry. The time got away from me," she said, acting confused, having been engrossed in her work.

He moved to her, placed the bottle gingerly on her desk then pushed her roughly back into the chair, shoving his face close to hers. His hot breath was within inches of her nose, and she could smell the whiskey.

His voice held a sneer. "Ah, the great writer, telling the wondrous story of Arizona."

She opened her mouth but said nothing, fearing a response would only make him angrier.

"You're here in this room all day, and you accomplish nothing of value as far as I can see. Why can't you be like my friends' wives and act more social? I need you out in the community, representing me in this land deal; you should be working in the thrift shop or serving on the board of the library. But no! The intellectual Kathleen is above all of that!"

She made no movement, hoping his anger would subside. He shifted his body slightly away from her, and she, in turn, wrongly judged he was going to drop the subject. She tried again to get out of the chair, but his anger exploded. A big man whose excesses in food and drink had caused him to develop a protruding stomach, Scott reach over and ripped open the front of her cotton blouse, his eyes moving to her breasts, showing white through her lace bra.

"You always had beautiful tits," Scott growled, shoving his hand inside the bra, fingering her nipples.

Frightened because her husband had never acted quite like this, Kathleen tried to gather her thoughts. Should she do nothing in the hope he would stop or would she be better off to show she was angry? Before she could decide, Scott pulled back, unzipped his pants and shoved himself into her mouth, jamming his body close to her face. She began to choke, but he grabbed her by the hair and held her face to his body as she struggled. Her struggling aroused him more and he moved faster until he climaxed. Her arms flailed helplessly against him as she gagged on the fluid. He let go of her and she leaned over, vomiting on the Mexican tile floor.

Shaking terribly, she slowly wiped her mouth with the back of her hand. After a few moments, she moved to cover her breasts, but he grabbed her by her upper arms and pulled her out of the chair.

"Stop it! Stop it!" she screamed, trying to break away from him. Instead, he reached up and hit her with his full open hand on the side of her head. A blinding pain rose out of her ear, and she could feel her own blood flow down the side of her face.

"I'm not through with you!"

Stunned by the blow, she gave him no fight as he pushed her hard to the floor. He yanked her cotton skirt up and pulled off her panties, becoming excited again at the sight of her.

She struggled to get out from under him, and in response, he hit her again, this time the blow was a clenched fist to her left shoulder, breaking her clavicle. A blinding flash of light came over Kathleen, and she passed out.

When she regained consciousness, the room was dark and cold. The house was silent except for the humming of her computer. Kathleen found herself face down on the tile floor amid her own vomit. Scott did to her what he always threatened during his drunken rages. She thanked God she could not remember, but the pain was searing, like a hot knife had been thrust into her bowels.

Now, hatred flooded over Kathleen her as she stared at her husband's coffin, thinking bitterly that the beloved Scott Buckley, pride of Sedona, beat and sodomized his wife, was a drunk and a womanizer.

She stiffened. Eight men leaned into the cold spring wind, carrying the bronze casket past her. All of them she knew well. None of them looked at her as they passed, carrying their heavy load up the incline into the church.

Kathleen felt a horrible dread. She knew instinctively how this day would go, yet for some unexplainable reason she felt the necessity to see the finish of Scott Buckley.

She brushed a tear away, angry that it might be taken by others as a show of grief. She turned to her mother and cousin.

"Maybe the pain will go away if I do this, stand through this agony of hearing what a wonderful man he was. God! Why did I put up with it?"

Charley's face was hard as he looked at the pious-looking men carrying Scott's remains. "Maybe we should go, Kathy. You don't need to go through this farce."

But she did, and she knew it. Kathleen shook her head, and her eyes were bright, unflinching. She grabbed Charley by the arm and then put her arm around her mother, and together they walked up the sidewalk and into the foyer of the church.

The smell of incense seemed to seep from the thick adobe walls. It was a sickening sweet smell, always reminding Kathleen of the difficulties of life as a Roman Catholic: walking into the confessional with the sin of hatred for her husband seeped into her soul, dreading telling the priest the same sin over and over again.

Long before the attack she gave up, both with the church and with Scott. Her husband didn't believe in marital counseling; he was wary of anyone in town knowing his marriage to Kathleen was less than it appeared, including the family priest.

As for Father Timothy O'Malley, he never confronted Scott after Kathleen's accusations of physical abuse, although she asked him once if he would talk to Scott after an especially trying confession. The priest's explanation was that both of them needed to see him in the formality of the rectory, an act that Kathleen and Father O'Malley knew Scott would never do. She did not ask again, just as she never entered the confessional again.

To Kathleen's way of thinking, the real reason the priest never confronted Scott was money. Once a year, at Easter, when Scott attended Mass for the consumption of the community and Father O'Malley, he would casually throw a $10,000 unfolded check into the basket. Everyone else who sat in the prestigious front pew saw Scott's generosity as the basket was passed from person to person, much to Kathleen's embarrassment. And at the end of Easter Mass, when the priest greeted his flock, Scott always received a hearty hug.

Standing in the foyer, Charley opened the doors to the church. Scott's casket, now covered in a dense blanket of scarlet roses, was already placed in front of the altar. The Buckley family sat firmly to the left of the casket, in the front pew she so despised.

Kathleen saw her step-daughters were dressed appropriately for once. Jessica, the eldest, usually wore skirts so short that no one really had to guess at her physical attributes. Natalie, the youngest, always wore the loose, colorful clothing of New Age devotees, but today she was dressed, as was her sister, in a dark, conservative suit. Kathleen guessed her brother-in-law, Philip, had something to do with the change in their appearance. As usual, he was dressed immaculately in a black, expensive business suit. The man had taste, Kathleen had to admit.

To the right sat the ushers, men of standing in the community, all of them Rotarians. In front of the ushers were dozens of flower arrangements, in every kind and hue, sent by officials throughout the state, including the governor of Arizona.

The flowers filled the front and sides of the altar, and the air was thick with the smell of them. One arrangement, placed to the side of the casket, was an exceptionally large wreath of red, white, and blue flowers in the form of the Presidential Seal of the United States. Kathleen smiled despite herself. Her brother-in-law's large yearly donations to the Democratic National Committee finally paid off.

Toward the right side of the church, back from the altar, four members of the Altar Society stood guarding two pews, blocking them off for Kathleen, her family and a few close friends, discretely away from the Buckleys. The men nodded to her as she walked toward them, moving back so she and her family could sit down.

Organ music played softly in the background, and Kathleen watched the church fill with Scott's friends and acquaintances. The funeral drew the cream of Sedona's society. Wealthy businessmen came dressed in dark suits, a far cry from their usual casual attire. They knew Scott from the years he served as president of the chamber of commerce. Their wives were dressed in spring finery despite the cold weather. They wore silk suits and dresses, expensive rings on their pampered hands.

Other mourners included land developers, real estate brokers, politicians, and community leaders. They spoke quietly, consoling each other over the tragedy of Scott's untimely death.

A few made an effort to seek out Kathleen. Irene Hemp, president of the taxpayers association, walked to Kathleen's pew, leaned over and gave her a hug.

"What a horrible shock! I can't believe it. Have the police told you anything?"

It was apparent the older woman had been crying. Her mascara was already smudged beneath her eyes.

"I was told he hit an ice pocket early Easter morning about 100 feet from the curve at the bridge near Tlaquepaque, lost control of the car and slammed into the railing. He died instantly." Kathleen's voice was low, controlled.

Irene shook her head. "Who would have thought Scott Buckley would die like that? My God, this town will never see another like him. No one will ever do what he did."

The dark humor of the comment crossed Kathleen's mind, but she remained silent. She dropped her eyes, fearing Irene would see her real feelings, but the other woman was engulfed in her own grief. As Irene moved away, Kathleen saw others glance at her. Many more ignored her, not looking in her direction even though she had known them for years. She was glad she wore the large black hat, and moved it closer around her face, physically and emotionally hiding in it.

But the hat afforded no privacy to the front of her. Jessica and Natalie Buckley turned and gave her a searing look of contempt. Scott's brother never turned, his straight back almost worse than the look from Kathleen's step-daughters.

In the pew in front of her, the chairman of the board of the Sedona-Oak Creek Bank sat down with his wife next to him. The Emersons, who owned a plush resort in Oak Creek Canyon, north of Sedona sat with them. They all saw her as they waited to be ushered into the pew, but despite years of friendship with Kathleen, none acknowledged her presence.

She pursed her lips to prevent herself from crying, not wanting these people to see she felt the sting of their deliberate snub. Kathleen's simmering anger began to take hold of her, but she was able to push it down, out of sight, just as she had for many years.

Several friends from the *Arizona Republic* sat down in the pew behind her. Despite their hectic work schedule at the largest newspaper in Arizona, they drove up from Phoenix in a show of support for Kathleen who garnered a plum reporting job on the paper after she left Scott.

Next to Rose sat Kathleen's best friend, Carrie Southern, a tall, blond woman, who spoke bluntly to Kathleen about everything in life. She never minced her words, and Kathleen loved her all the more for that quality.

Impeccably dressed in a brown linen suit, accented with a large brown straw hat, Carrie reached across Rose to pat Kathleen on the hand and gave her a loving look.

"Hey, kid. You can get through this."

Kathleen nodded and gave Carrie a wan smile. Through the years, there was nothing they had not discussed, from the latest gossip enveloping Sedona to the loneliness and despair of difficult marriages.

Sitting on the other side of Charley was Marlene Fisher, the neighbor Kathleen fled to after Scott's attack. Marlene had a gaudy way about her, wearing as much diamond jewelry as her svelte body could carry, but Kathleen knew she had a good heart.

Kathleen put her arm through Charley's and held his rough hand. A carpenter by trade, his hand, despite the calluses, was the most soothing she ever felt. Kathleen confided in Charlie ever since she could remember, everything from her girlhood dreams of becoming a newspaper reporter to her sudden decision late in life to give up her career to marry Scott.

"I'm so glad you're here." Her hands were shaking.

Charley leaned over to Kathleen, avoiding the brim of her hat and looked into her eyes that were beginning to tear.

"Don't cry, Kathy. He was nothing but a bastard to you. He's not worth your grief."

"I think that's why I am crying. There's so much, Charley, so much hatred and despair in me because of...of, you know! And now, you see how his friends, our friends, act like I was some kind of leper because I left him."

"But it can only get better for you now. Just think, you won't have to go through a bitter divorce, which you dreaded. He's dead, caused by his own hand. You're alive, and you have your whole life ahead of you."

"God, Charley, what an optimist you are!"

He laughed softly. "I know. I wish you were too."

At that moment, behind them, a woman moved into the pew next to Kathleen's friends from the newspaper. A man from the Altar Society came over to notify her that the pew was reserved for Kathleen. Red-headed and in her mid-thirties, she spoke loud enough for everyone in the surrounding pews to hear.

"I don't give a damn if this is reserved for her! I'm a good friend of the Buckley family and there isn't any place else to sit!"

She spoke in a menacing tone as she pushed herself some space by planting her large purse between herself and Kathleen's editor, Rebecca Adams, who was forced to move closer to a coworker.

Kathleen turned to see who invaded her reserved pew and quickly turned back, feeling as if she'd been knifed. The woman was one of Scott's whores, Elizabeth Ashton, resplendent in black, as if she were the widow, not Kathleen.

Through years of habit, a quick prayer flew to Kathleen's lips. "Dear God, please, get me through this!"

CHAPTER 2

T he funeral Mass began, and as it did, Kathleen swore silently, damning Scott's soul to hell and feeling the tear in her own being for doing it. Despite her efforts to forget the past, her hatred blossomed and finally surfaced: She could not stop weeping.

Charley put his arm around her, drawing her close; she took off her hat and buried her head in his shoulder, trying to stifle her sobs. The rise and fall of the prayers murmured for Scott's soul filled her with desolation, and Kathleen felt herself lose control, shaking with the violence of her emotion. Those sitting in front of her moved uneasily in their pew as they heard Kathleen, some of them turning to look at her.

"Kathy!" Charley whispered, shaking her a little. "Get hold of yourself."

Kathleen took a deep breathe, trying to muffle her sobs. After a few minutes, the tears stopped, but the shaking did not. Charley clutched her tighter to him until she began to calm down, and as she did, she focused her attention toward the front of the church.

St. John Vianney's altar was as striking as the outside scenery. The large cross, attached to the wall directly behind the priest, looked like intertwined tree branches. At the base of the cross were trails of ivy growing through a mound of Sedona's red rocks, giving the cross the appearance that it was freestanding.

To the right side of the cross was a life-sized figure of Christ, complete with nail marks in the figure's hands and feet. The design of the altar reflected

Sedona's art colony, but there was no feeling here for Kathleen of an intimacy with God.

The first half of the Mass finished and Father O'Malley began his eulogy. Kathleen placed her hat back on her head, hoping it would provide some semblance of privacy.

"Scott Buckley was the best of Sedona," the priest said with a hint of his Irish brogue that made him such a favorite at social events frequented by Sedona's wealthy. No one could tell a joke better than Father O'Malley. At those affairs, the lanky priest's thick blond hair would fall forward into his eyes as he imbibed a little too much of the fine Irish whisky offered him.

"This man wasn't just a businessman or Sedona's best unofficial promoter. He was Sedona. There wasn't a morning that he couldn't be seen at Friendly Bob's Restaurant, drinking coffee and dreaming up ways to make Sedona better. He was responsible for the kind of close-knit loving community we live in today."

Kathleen raised her eyes to look at the priest and wondered for a moment why he would throw in such an untruth, but then she looked over at the ushers and saw the collection baskets in their hands.

The priest continued after letting his last comment sink in.

"When he came here in 1964 and opened Buckley Hardware, Scott envisioned a community where all could benefit from the beauty of the red rocks, where business would flourish and where there would be schools, parks, and recreation for its residents. He envisioned a city that would draw thousands of tourists, yet remain small—a hometown community for the people who live here. And he worked to make that city a reality.

"Scott cared. Not only about Sedona, but about his family. He alone raised his two daughters, Jessica and Natalie, after the untimely death of his first wife, Morgan."

The priest put his eyes down. Morgan's suicide was a scandalous episode that the priest was able to keep from the ears of the community because of his influence with Sedona's sheriff.

Although nothing was ever said between them, Father O'Malley knew Scott's large Easter donation to the church was not given out of the goodness of his heart.

"Scott was a beloved father to his daughters and an adoring son to his parents, who are no longer living. He was also close to his brother, Philip, who will be taking over the family's financial enterprises."

Father O'Malley took a deep breath, audible over the church microphone. "He was also beloved by his second wife, Kathleen."

Kathleen jerked her head up to look at the priest. She saw an involuntary movement from Philip Buckley at the sound of her name, and Jessica and Natalie whispered to one another.

A momentary smile came to Kathleen. Her personal opinion of Timothy O'Malley was that he spent his time away from the altar soothing the wealthy egos of his parish. She was surprised by his show of intestinal fortitude.

The priest paused and looked over the well-heeled crowd. "Scott Buckley will be deeply missed by this community. He can never be replaced."

The Mass moved into the last stage, with many in the church stepping forward to accept Holy Communion, including the Buckleys.

But Kathleen did not get up. She sat, looking straight ahead. Her expression hardened as she watched her husband's family piously communing with God despite their adulteries and cunning business deals.

There stood her brother-in-law, Philip, standing straight as an arrow, holding out his hands to receive the symbolic body of Christ. Kathleen knew Philip's sudden sanctity was only for show. Even Scott, who took great pride in swinging a sweet deal whenever he could, was suspicious of Philip.

Then there was Jessica, whose string of well-muscled paid-off studs was the constant talk of Sedona. Kathleen once heard Jessica referred to as the slut of Sedona, a comment that did not surprise her considering Jessica's voracious sexual appetite.

And then there was Natalie. Kathleen marveled how easily her youngest step daughter could receive communion when everyone in the community knew she left the church years ago to embrace New Age philosophies.

A wash of hopelessness enveloped Kathleen. The Buckleys only worship at their own temples, she thought. Only money and power make a difference to them, not God.

As the crowd began to leave the church, Kathleen stayed in her pew with Charley and her mother, not wanting to talk to anyone. Her friends from the newspaper offered their condolences, and Carrie and Marlene said they would wait outside for her.

When the church emptied, the three of them walked up to the closed casket. Kathleen brushed the side of it with her hand, noting how cold it was, like the body inside. She stood there for a moment, reflecting on her life with Scott Buckley.

Despite all the outward appearances of being married to a wealthy, charming man, it had been an empty, loveless life. Feeling exhausted, she realized the years spent with him were wasted, leaving no real meaning. The countless social events to raise money for the local symphony or arts center, the dinner parties to impress some big shot, and the political machinations behind the scene that were so important to Scott brought nothing of import to the grave.

All she wanted for herself was to find peace. She felt shamed by her behavior during Mass, crying uncontrollably, not for Scott, but for herself. Kathleen silently vowed that she would never cry like that again.

"Let's get out of here," she said to her family.

As they walked outside, Father O'Malley stood alone by the door. The priest seemed hesitant to approach her, so she walked up to him.

"Thanks, Father, for mentioning my name. I know that was a hard thing for you to do, considering the mere mention of my existence might affect Philip Buckley's donation to the church."

"Kathleen..." the priest began, but she cut him off.

"Never mind, Father. I don't need any explanations. If anyone knows how things work in this town, I do."

CHAPTER 3

Philip Buckley looked around Enchantment Resort's dining room. It was not the coziest dining room in Sedona, but that was exactly why he chose the secluded retreat for this meeting with his two nieces. He hoped the elegance of the room would remind them what money brings and that the flawless service would prompt them to act with a modicum of grace and dignity, qualities they usually lacked. Besides, Philip was uneasy in cozy settings.

The Enchantment, a spectacular resort nestled in Boynton Canyon about five miles from the heart of Sedona, was filled with tourists this time of year. That was the other reason he picked this site. Philip knew there would be little chance of anyone from within the community lunching there.

Philip specifically requested a table at the far end of the room, next to the window. He took a quick, cursory glance at the stark formations of red rock outside the dining room window, but carefully eyed all who came into the dining area as he sipped his gin and tonic. Philip never did understand all the excitement about Sedona's red rocks. He would have preferred to be in the glass and steel Buckley corporate building in downtown Phoenix for this meeting, but time was of the essence. He knew he would never be able to get Jessica and Natalie to Phoenix on the same day.

Amid the tourists in their shorts and T-shirts, Philip looked out of place. He was carefully dressed in his usual business attire: a conservative black suit, white long-sleeved monogrammed shirt, and dark tie. His coal-black hair and mustache was carefully trimmed. He sat ram-rod straight in the cushioned chair, searching for his brother's daughters.

"Ah, here you are," he said as the pair finally arrived. He did not rise to greet them on purpose, but instead gave a quick smile, which faded to his usual expression of no expression at all.

Philip was the opposite of his dead brother. Scott, like a snake charmer, could mesmerize both male and female alike with his soothing voice, wit, and warm smile. Philip's personality was more like the snake charmer's cobra, cunning and deadly. Today, however, he promised himself to act more like Scott.

Jessica looked at her uncle as she settled into her seat, plopping her large Gucci handbag on the floor next to the table.

"Why have you asked us to have lunch all the way out here? I had to curtail my tennis lessons at the racquet club. We could have had lunch there, Philip." A touch of anger rose in her voice as she emphasized her uncle's name.

She was dressed in a white tennis outfit, which was designed to show off her sexy athletic figure. A matching tennis cap held back her short coif. She wore three tennis bracelets, two studded with diamonds and the other sparkling with deep blue sapphires to match her large diamond and sapphire ring.

"I have some business to discuss with you, and I felt the racquet club has too many people listening." Philip emphasized his remark by speaking in a tone low enough that Jessica had to lean over to hear him.

Natalie nudged her sister.

"Oh, Jessica! Quit your negativity. This is just fine, Uncle Philip. It's been a long time since I've been here. I should come out more often to feel the wonderful energy in Boynton Canyon, but I usually grab a protein drink at the health food store."

Natalie was dressed in a long, colorful skirt and a T-shirt that hung over her hips. Around her neck was an exquisite amethyst crystal, laced with small gemstones. Long, beaded earrings dangled from her ears, catching in her long hair.

Philip eyed his nieces. He wondered how two women raised in the same family could be so different. He would have to watch his step with these two exactly because of their differences. With Jessica, he knew he could be blunt, but not so with Natalie, who always looked at the worldview in such discussions.

The waiter caught Philips's eye and quickly came to the table. He took their drink order.

"I'm disappointed to see you playing tennis, Jessica, so soon after your father's funeral. What will people say?" His voice was smooth as velvet.

Her response was quick and pointed. "To hell with what people say! Besides, everyone knows I never got along with Daddy anyway—and I never got along with you either."

"That's exactly why I've called you both here today. Despite the fact that we're not exactly a loving family, we need one another now. We need to discuss what's going to happen with your father's will, the forest-exchange property, such as that. It's important we present to the community the impression we are grieving over your father, drunken bastard that he was.

Perceptions count...I know you know that, Jessica dear."

"Don't 'Jessica dear' me! I know what you're up to. We're going to contest the will because Kathleen has been left one-fourth of the property. You want us to look like the grief-stricken family who has to share Daddy's fortune with a cunt that left him in his hour of greatest need."

"That's about right, Jessica. I'm glad to see you have a handle on the situation. Natalie, do you understand that we need to contest the will?" His tone continued to be smooth, obsequious.

Natalie did not look directly at Philip. She looked down at the tablecloth and fingered the crystal around her neck.

"I don't like any of this. It's bad karma."

Jessica cut in the conversation and leaned over toward her sister. "How the hell are you going to live without dear Daddy's money? Or would you just like to camp out in the forest like some of your New Age friends in one of those filthy, beat-up camper trucks filled with their every belonging? Better yet, maybe you would like to be one of those matted-haired lunatics seeking God who walk through Sedona with their backpack clung to them like it's a second skin?"

"If I have to do that, then I will. I know I have lived off of Daddy's money. Maybe Daddy's death is the lesson I'm supposed to learn in this life, not to live off of others. I probably need to meditate on that for a while." Natalie sounded like a little girl.

Jessica exploded, "Christ! Just talking to you makes my blood boil. Why don't you act like a normal person instead of using all that New Age bullshit psychobabble?"

Natalie sat up straight like a puppet whose stings had just been yanked. She turned to look directly at her older sister, her voice quivering but surprisingly strong. "I'm tired of listening to you attack what I believe in, Jessica. How about your lifestyle? Let's look at that for a moment. During the day all you do is play tennis, lunch or shop. At night, you screw any man you can get your hands on. At least I'm trying to understand myself and the meaning of life. You're nothing but a whore!"

"Shut-up!" Philip said as the waiter approached with their drinks. All three picked up their menus while the waiter set down another gin and tonic for Philip, a Perrier with lime for Jessica, and Rim Rock water for Natalie.

After they ordered and the waiter left the table, Philip leaned forward on his elbows and gave the two women a hard stare. His tone was even, measured.

"Look. I don't give a good goddamn about either of you. As far as I'm concerned you can both go to hell, but we're in this together. Your father made a change in his will about a year before he died, probably while he was in one of his remorseful periods. Prior to that, she was never included in the will. The prenuptial agreement Kathleen signed prevented her from getting anything from the estate."

Jessica squeezed the lime into her drink. "So...what's the strategy to cut Kathleen out?"

"To prove your father was an alcoholic and not in his right mind when he changed the will."

Natalie shook her head and Jessica rudely laughed. "And you're the one who's talking about perceptions! People in this community aren't going to take that one lightly."

Philip pressed on, unconcerned.

"What really disturbs me is the land trade. Those Forest Service bureaucrats are hard enough to deal with, let alone working with them while the land is in contested probate."

Natalie again shook her head. "I don't understand anything about this land exchange."

Jessica interrupted. "All I know is that Daddy bought acreage along Oak Creek many years ago from some old geezer who was down on his luck and needed money. What is it anyway, Philip?"

Philip looked around him, making sure no one was within earshot. He explained Forest Service policy was to trade their FS land that borders development with land the agency considers valuable.

"We're talking about trading the ten acres your father owned along Oak Creek for one hundred acres the Forest Service owns near Edgarville. You know, that small rural community south of Sedona."

"So, what's the big problem?" Natalie asked her uncle.

"The problem is that these Sedona environmental do-gooders don't want the Forest Service to deal in land exchanges. They know the Edgarville land will be developed by us, and those people who live out there don't want anyone else out there. They like that rural bullshit with their horses and flies. I hear they're a strange bunch, angry with the government for every goddamn thing. This is a very touchy political issue."

The waiter delivered their lunches. Philip picked at his Caesar salad.

"Your father would have never gone for the land exchange idea except that he was negotiating with high-placed government officials before he died. They expressed interest in buying outright the Edgarville property. They were talking about it being used for some kind of government project."

"What kind of government project?" Natalie asked, a note of concern in her voice.

Jessica cut in, her voice as sharp as the knife she used to cut her rare steak sandwich.

"Don't worry, Natalie. There's no place out there in Edgarville where your friends do their mumbo jumbo," referring to the Native American medicine wheels New Agers build out of rocks and use for meditation ceremonies.

"Go to hell," Natalie answered her sister in a low tone.

Philip growled. "Stop it! Nothing will happen out there that will be of any consequence to either of you."

He was growing tired of the constant argument between them. What would it take to convince them to agree to discredit their father's reputation enough to get the will changed?

Philip watched Natalie bite into her vegetarian quiche. She seemed to savor every tidbit. He knew from what she said before that she enjoyed good food and loved the surroundings of the posh resort. Despite her New Age spiritual and environmental leanings, Philip knew Natalie needed money to continue to live like she did, playing at the New Age game, but living outside the quirkiness of it.

Jessica sliced up her steak sandwich, devouring the red meat like she devoured men. Philip also knew Jessica could never live a life without wealth. Her high-priced sexual haunts demanded such resources.

Suddenly, Jessica put her fork down, addressing her uncle. "What would be the difference between splitting the estate three ways to four?"

Philip considered the question before he answered. "Like traveling first class on the Concorde compared to tourist class on any domestic airline."

There was silence as the two women considered the alternative. Surprisingly, Natalie was the first to respond. "What can I do to help?"

Jessica also nodded, understanding the financial implications.

Philip smiled for the first time. It seemed his nieces did understand more than vortex meditation sites and sex.

"Look...this is the story. Scott was an alcoholic, but a contributing member of Sedona society. He loved Sedona and was president of the chamber, you name it and he was involved.

Still, alcoholism had him by the throat and for some unknown reason while under the influence, he changed his will. All of that will be documented to the court. I just want to make sure you both agree to it."

Jessica was still worried. "Say for instance we can't convince the judge about Daddy's alcoholism and Kathleen inherits one-fourth of the estate. Can't she stop the exchange of the property if she owns part of it?"

"No. Your father named me the estate's executor, and I can do what I believe to be in the best interest of all the heirs. That would include the land exchange whether Kathleen likes it or not. I'm quite sure as a reporter Kathleen is no longer living in the lap of luxury. Certainly, Kathleen has a practical side."

Philip paid the bill with his American Express Gold Card, leaving the waiter a large tip in the hopes he would not repeat anything he might have heard. As he followed his nieces out of the dining room, he inwardly laughed because of their petty concerns about Kathleen.

Don't worry, ladies, Philip thought. I'll make certain Kathleen gets what she deserves.

CHAPTER 4

The gravel crackled under the tires of Kathleen's car as she drove into Sedona Memorial Cemetery.

Kathleen looked around her. God, this is barren, she thought.

She remembered the large cemeteries in her home state of California, with their massive beds of roses and statues of Jesus Christ, His arms open as if gathering in His flock. Even though Kathleen felt the religious aspect was a bit contrived, the graveyards there somehow gave a sense of comfort to the living.

But this cemetery was different. Here, the wind howled through the juniper trees, and the sound echoed back from the high red rock cliffs at the edge of the graveyard. There was no comfort here, only the raw elements of nature.

As she drove slowly through the cemetery, she noticed grave sites encased in short brick or red rock stone walls, showing off faded silk flowers stuck in the red dusty earth to commemorate those who lay beneath. Other grave sites looked well-kept with decorative rock placed inside the walls, holding down the red dust. Junipers dotted the area, adding the only green to mute the stark rust-colored ground.

Kathleen drove to the end of the road to the Buckley grave site. She parked in front of the well-built red rock wall imbedded with a bronze plaque. The name Buckley stood out in capital letters.

She sat for a moment staring at the name so revered in Sedona. It was June, two months since Scott's funeral and this was her first visit to his grave.

She wanted to come sooner but was afraid to face his death and all that it meant to her life.

Kathleen got out of her car and paused before climbing up the steps to Scott's grave, surveying the surrounding area. This was the last grave site in the cemetery, next to the area where vaults hold cremated remains. A large tin shed stood off to the left and a piece of metal from the shed rattled in the wind, making the cemetery sound as forlorn as it looked.

She climbed up the three steps, not wanting to do what she knew she must—confront her loathing. Despite her feeling of shame at her behavior at Scott's funeral, Kathleen hoped her emotional release there would make her feel whole again, but it had not. Perhaps, she could shuck off this passion here, and lay her malice to rest along with Scott.

The Buckleys had buried four of their own here: Helen and Lawrence Buckley, Scott's parents. Morgan Buckley, Scott's first wife, lay next to Scott. A slight pang of jealousy flickered in Kathleen, despite her animosity. She wondered where she was supposed to lay when she was dead. On the other side of Scott? Not likely.

On Scott's bronze grave marker was his full name, Scott Lawrence Buckley. The marker underneath read, "Received into the Lord's loving care."

Kathleen felt a twinge of surprise when she read it. Could that possibly be true considering the life he led? She did not think beyond that momentary wonder and bent down, running her hand over the marker, remembering.

She fell hard for Scott, changed her life to have him for her husband by moving to Sedona after a romantic two-month courtship, abruptly ending her newspaper career at the *Los Angeles Times*. But soon after the marriage, after the initial euphoria, she realized she made a disastrous mistake.

The adoring, fondling lover who publicly kissed her passionately on the mouth was often impotent as his drinking escalated. And with the drinking came the violence—from a sharp punch to her arm, to the attack the night she left him.

The longer she was married to Scott, the more she realized what a bastard he was, particularly in his attitude toward her. Scott knew how to make Kathleen feel like a married whore, doling out money when the mood struck him. If she did a particularly good job hosting one of his political dinner parties, Scott would leave several hundred dollars next to her bedside table just as if she'd favored him sexually.

When he first did it, about a year after their marriage, she was puzzled, and asked him if he put the money on the table by accident.

He smiled his dazzling smile. "No, it's for you. You did a nice job handling those political assholes from the county. They think they can sweet talk me out of pushing for Sedona becoming a city. It may take a few more years, but I'll make sure it happens."

"I did a nice job? Why are you giving me money when all I did was act like your wife?" There was anger in her voice.

"It's insurance, baby; insurance. Just to make sure you stay on my side." He pulled her to him, kissed her hard, fondling her breast.

Kathleen crumpled the money in her fist. "Honest to God, Scott! Sometimes you're such a son of a bitch. I don't want your goddamn money anyway. Not like that! Not like I'm some whore. I'm your wife, remember?"

He shrugged his shoulders as if he did not understand her anger. "Do as you please. If you like, I'll give the money instead to Jessica or Natalie."

Scott knew that would raise Kathleen's anger to a fevered pitch. Instead, Kathleen placed the crumpled money on Scott's dresser.

"If you want to treat your daughters like the whores they are, that's your business," was her level-voiced response.

Scott's smile never changed, but he grabbed her by the elbow and squeezed hard, hard enough to bring tears to her eyes.

"My daughters know how to fuck for pleasure and for profit. I don't think you know how to do either, Kathleen. That's what comes from being too good a Catholic." He laughed. It was a nasty sound, humiliating her.

Kathleen yanked her arm from him and he walked into the other room to get his usual nightcap from the bar.

She went into the kitchen and put an ice pack on her elbow, knowing she would have to wear long sleeves for two weeks to cover the bruise.

Standing now at his grave, Kathleen thought about Scott's game to control her. While she looked like his wife, with the expensive dresses, jewelry, and world-wide jaunts, in reality she was a financial pauper except for her own savings from the sale of her former home in California.

Kathleen owned nothing that was Scott's. The prenuptial agreement she signed before their wedding gave sole ownership of his home, hardware business, shopping centers, and other real estate properties to him. Nothing was ever bought or owned jointly during their marriage.

She sighed, remembering the pressure Scott and his lawyer put on her that day. She was tired and wanted to be done with this legal business. Tomorrow they were boarding a plane that would take them to San Juan, Puerto Rico, where they would be married the next day. She still had to pack and shop for a few more clothes.

Kathleen heard Puerto Rico was a beautiful place, with its sunny beaches, tropical rain forest, and large Spanish fortress. She thought it would be romantic to be married in the big cathedral that sits in the heart of old San Juan, but the arrangements had been time consuming and difficult to make in such a short time. Everything seemed so rushed. Now, this prenuptial agreement came out of the blue. Scott never discussed it with her before that morning.

Her hand shook a little as she signed the document. Kathleen knew she was blinded by a love for Scott that flooded over her late in life. The intensity of her feelings surprised her; she felt as if her heart would stop if she had to spend one moment without him. On that day, she did not dare see his financial manipulation of her.

"Goddamn him anyway. He never did anything he promised, the lying son-of-a-bitch. But he sure as hell knew how to make it sound like he would!"

She bent down and rubbed her hand in the red dirt along side the grave marker as if she could reach down and touch him beneath the soil. She wanted to give up her feeling of hatred for him, but she realized as she touched the earth that she did not know how to let loose of it. It had become so much a part of her now.

Although the earth was dry, its powdery rust-colored form still stained her hand and clung under her fingernails. She tried to brush the stain away, but in doing so she accidentally rubbed her hand on the side of her white slacks, making a mark that would be difficult, if not impossible, to get out.

"It's like it infects your soul," she said in disgust, giving up the task.

She stood, and swept her hand across her eyes, determined not to cry; instead she smudged her face with the red dirt. Kathleen felt anger flood into her soul, as memories of the past poured pain on her unhealed wounds.

She brushed at her pants in one more desperate effort, shook her head, and walked down the steps to her car, opened the door and stood for a moment, staring at the Buckley name so prominently displayed.

The hardness of her hatred welled up inside her throat, making her feel as if she was going to choke on it. How could she be rid of it, put it aside, get on with her life?

A thought came to Kathleen, something from many years before when she was doing an article on a psychiatric counselor who worked with abused women. She asked the counselor how abused women could work through the hatred they harbored for those who hurt them.

"The act of forgiveness seems to do it for some," the counselor told Kathleen. "But for others, that's not possible. In that case, I tell them that instead of giving up their hatred, they need to use it instead."

At the time, it was an answer Kathleen did not quite understand.

"Use it?"

"Yes. Turn it around. I tell the women who come to me that if they can't get rid of it, use the hatred to get where they want to go in their life."

Kathleen considered what the counselor told her. She knew her hatred kept her alive since Scott's attack, had even helped her get through the ordeal of his death. Maybe putting it aside was something she would never be able to do.

She stood for a long time with that thought and then faced Scott's resting place.

Alone in the cemetery with only the wind as a companion, she said aloud, "You're not going to get me, Scott. You tried when you were alive. I'll be damned if you'll do it from the grave."

CHAPTER 5

Kathleen left the cemetery and drove toward the bridge at Tlaquepaque, the spot where Scott was killed. She slowed down as she came to the sharp curve, and noticed the new portion of bridge structure. A cold chill came over her as she drove across, and she suddenly wondered if it were true that a person's spirit remains near the spot where they violently die.

Her thoughts caused her to miss the two cobblestone entrances into Tlaquepaque, a Hispanic-styled arts and craft village filled with dozens of expensive shops and art galleries.

Traffic was heavy on Highway 179 with summer tourists, so Kathleen turned left at Portal Lane, the entrance to Los Abrigados Resort, an exclusive hotel and health spa located behind Tlaquepaque. She found a shady parking spot to the left in the area used by hotel and shop employees and spent a moment to remove the smudge of dirt from her face.

Tlaquepaque never failed to delight Kathleen with its beautifully-planted gardens and fountains. Large sycamores draped the adobe courtyards and formed intricate shadows on the tiled walkways. While in the shaded coolness of its ivy-covered passageways, she always felt a sense of being elsewhere, like the heart of Mexico. During those times when she needed escape from her troubles, Kathleen would often come to Tlaquepaque and listen to the happy sounds of tourists delighted with the beauty of the place.

Rene At Tlaquepaque, a French restaurant, was a particular favorite of Kathleen's. The restaurant's cozy country French atmosphere gave it a sense of intimacy, and its reputation for fine food pulled in a clientele of wealthy residents and tourists. Kathleen decided to splurge on herself and meet Carrie Southern at Rene's for lunch. She found Carrie at the bar drinking an Irish coffee.

"Hi, kid." Carrie climbed down from the tall stool. She gave Kathleen a hug and then put her at arm's length to look at her. "You look a hell of a lot better than you did last time I saw you."

Carrie's blond hair was pulled back from her face with a silver barrette. She wore a long pleated silk skirt in pale blue with a matching blouse. A large silver Concho belt cinched her thin waist, and she accented the belt with dangling silver earrings.

Kathleen suddenly felt she did not dress appropriately for the luncheon, and was particularly aware of her dirt-stained slacks. But before Kathleen could answer her friend, she saw that the host, Andre, hovered nearby. Kathleen turned to him.

"Hello, Andre. How have you been?" She extended her hand.

"Mrs. Buckley! It's so good to see you. May I offer my condolences about the death of your husband. We miss him...and you, of course." He took her hand in both of his and gently squeezed them.

Rene's had always been a special place for Scott and Kathleen, but as the years of their marriage wore on both of them, Scott began taking other women there as well. Kathleen was grateful for Andre's savoir faire regarding Scott's indiscretions, smiling warmly in response to him. She then quickly asked if they could have a quiet table, "perhaps one of the booths."

"Most certainly. Right this way." He gave a small bow.

He led them through a large room filled with cloth-covered tables, into a narrow side room with cozy leather booths lined up on each wall. As she scooted into the booth, Kathleen wondered how Western art could fit so nicely with lace curtains and French country decor.

"If there is anything I can do, madam, please call upon me."

Kathleen thanked Andre as she slid into the booth. "This place was among Scott's favorites, but I wasn't in the mood to eat at one of the coffee shops in West Sedona," Kathleen said after Andre left.

Carrie tried to reassure her. "It's all right, Kathy. You have to face those memories sometime. You might as well do it now."

"You know there's a part of me that doesn't ever want to face it. I want to hide from it, go someplace where no one knows who I am."

"Yeah, well, Kathy, you did that. You moved to Phoenix when you left Scott. Did it help any? Did the pain of it go away or is it still stuck in your craw?"

Kathleen laughed at her good friend. "Jesus, Carrie! You do have a way of getting to the heart of things."

She took a sip of water. The handsome young waiter, dressed in a tuxedo shirt and black slacks, smiled as he approached the table.

"Good afternoon, ladies. May I tell you the luncheon specials?"

Kathleen half listened to the list of fresh fish and French dishes. She sat facing the main dining room and scanned the faces of people dining while the waiter rattled off the specials.

Most of the diners were tourists, but better attired than those who drive into town for the day dressed in shorts, T-shirts and fanny packs on their way to the Grand Canyon. Those who usually ventured into this restaurant wore casual, expensive clothes and were spending a few days in the area. There were even some diners dressed in formal business attire, obviously having lunch while discussing some business deal. Kathleen knew several of them.

At a table in the main dining room, there was a man Kathleen judged to be in his mid-thirties having lunch with the chairman of the board of the Sedona-Oak Creek Bank, Erwin Stanley. Kathleen had known Stanley for many years and she remembered with a pang that he and his wife, Judy, sat in the pew in front of her at Scott's funeral without acknowledging her. On the left side of Stanley sat Harold Winn, the president of the bank.

Winn was a short man with a large balding spot in the middle of his head. He tried to cover the glaring site by combing the few strands of gray hair at the front of his brow over his baldness, creating a sort of pompadour that had been in style in the 1940s.

Kathleen considered Harold Winn a weasel. She went to him for a personal bank loan when she left Scott, thinking that since she had known him for so many years he would give her a little leeway on the loan application.

Sitting behind his big desk in his plush office with a view that overlooked the red rocks, Winn casually asked her what her assets were. When she told him she owned none of Scott's properties because of the prenup agreement, he raised his eyebrows ever so slightly and then matter-of-factly told her she needed a co-signer for the $10,000 loan.

The interest rate was twenty percent, Winn said because she personally owned nothing of worth to the bank. When Kathleen suggested her jewels and furs, he was abrupt. "Real property is what this bank wants for collateral, Kathleen. Nothing else. You were stupid to sign that prenup agreement."

He ran his hand through his sparse strands of hair and a few beads of sweat showed on his shiny forehead. He patted them off with his silk handkerchief, puffing a little as if he had run some sort of race.

In desperation, Kathleen turned to Carrie and her husband, Ned. The couple took her in while she recuperated from Scott's attack, and they also willingly co-signed the loan.

Kathleen began to feel she had picked the wrong restaurant for lunch. She put her eyes down as all three men looked over at her. Erwin was saying something about her to the man she did not recognize. In desperation, she turned her attention to ordering from the sumptuous menu. After the waiter left, Carrie reached over and patted Kathleen's hand.

"I said you look better than you did at the funeral. But that was a truly awful day. Are you really better?"

Kathleen thought a moment before she answered. "I don't know, Carrie. I manage to do my work at the *Republic*, but with little enthusiasm. I feel as if I've lost something that I had as a young reporter. I guess I thought I was doing something good for society—reporting to the world the inequities of the system, the injustices that government throws at the average guy on the street. I don't think readers give a damn any more about those people who have fallen through the cracks of modern life. All they want is the sensationalism of the moment, the ten-second sound bite that feeds the public the misconception that the world is manageable."

"Maybe it's you who doesn't give a damn," was Carrie's off-the-cuff reply.

Kathleen absorbed Carrie's remark for a moment. "No. My lack of passion is because I'm trying to sort myself out, trying to understand the person who lived as the wife of Scott Buckley, bound by the Roman Catholic Church to do my duty. I have these two people in me, Carrie—one is this hard-boiled reporter and the other is this...this obedient, subservient wife. I don't know how in the name of God I shook off one role so casually and put on the other."

Carrie looked Kathleen straight in the eyes. "I think you're being too hard on yourself. Everyone has parts of different personalities in them, Kathy. Be a little forgiving of yourself and your sins. So what if you fell in love with a charming, rich man, and he turned out to be a bastard and you learned to loathe him? Do you think you're supposed to pay for that mistake, that error in judgment, all of your life?"

"I don't know; I guess I haven't resolved that yet."

"With who, yourself or God?" Carrie asked pointedly.

She was about to answer when the waiter, still smiling, interrupted them with their lunch. Kathleen had ordered lush crab crepes covered with a white sauce, and Carrie's dish was succulent lamb stew simmered in herbs and spices.

Over lunch, two fattening deserts, and steaming black coffee, they chatted mainly about Carrie's two teenage daughters, the gossip at the Sedona school district where Carrie worked as administrative assistant to the superintendent, and her upcoming vacation in Hawaii.

Finally, Carrie set down her fork and put her elbows on the table, leaning toward Kathleen.

"Look, Kathy. I think what you need is to find yourself a good man, someone who will love you and care for you. You never had that in Scott. You never had that in anybody. All you've ever had is that damn career of yours."

Kathleen could not help but laugh at Carrie's remark. "Ah, the good man theme! I wasn't very good at that game, Carrie. To me, all that's left is my career."

"Well, then, go after it again if that's what you want! Quit dawdling! Maybe you should go work for one of those big-time newspapers on the East Coast."

Kathleen smiled. "No, what I really dream about is running a small newspaper. Be the editor, reporter...the whole shebang."

For a second, her thoughts flew back to when she was in college and worked summers as a copy editor for a small newspaper in the Los Angeles suburbs. The editor, who was also the only reporter on the paper, was a cranky old woman. Kathleen remembered subscribers loved her or hated her, but they never ignored her. She did not understand why the vision of that woman stayed with her for thirty years, creating a longing she could not explain.

The waiter arrived with the bill. It was $52.

Carrie laughed as she dug out her wallet. "I'm going to have to starve the rest of the week to pay for this."

"I know, Carrie, but we don't get together that..." Kathleen's sentence dribbled off as the man who had been sitting at the table with Harold Winn and Erwin Stanley walked over to her table.

"Excuse me, Mrs. Buckley?"

"Yes?"

"My name is Jack Berens. I would like to talk to you sometime soon at your pleasure. I'd like to leave my business card with you, if you don't mind."

"What is this about?" A tone of suspicion crept into Kathleen's voice.

"I have a new business in Sedona and would like to discuss the possibility of your working for me."

"Mr. Berens..." Kathleen's voice trailed off as she looked at his business card. It read, "Jack Berens, publisher, *Sedona Chronicle*."

"Jack. Please call me Jack. I know who you are Mrs. Buckley. You're Kathleen Sullivan. You've worked for the *Los Angeles Times* and now the *Arizona Republic*. You're a fine reporter but you've been wasting your talents. This is a growing area. There's so much going on here that isn't being covered properly, and I think you can do that for the *Sedona Chronicle*. I think you can make an impact here. Call me."

Without another word, Jack Berens left the table and walked out of the restaurant. The two bankers followed him, both nodding to her as they left.

Kathleen looked again at the business card and put it in her purse.

Carrie smiled. "Hey, Kathy. Maybe this is the answer you've been looking for."

"I don't know. Coming back to Sedona would be difficult. In fact, it would be more than difficult."

Carrie looked at Kathleen for a moment, and responded quietly but forcefully.

"How's that famous saying go, Kathy? All things are difficult before they are easy."

Kathleen laughed. "Yeah, but the guy who said that never lived in Sedona."

CHAPTER 6

A week later, intrigued by Jack Berens' impassioned speech at the restaurant and pushed by Carrie's prompting, Kathleen walked in the door of his newspaper.

The office was located in the heart of Uptown Sedona, smack in the middle of tourist traffic and next door to one of the Jeep tour offices. On the south side of the *Chronicle* office were several shops sporting postcards of the red rocks, Sedona T-shirts, cactus jelly, and fake rattlesnake eggs.

As Kathleen stepped inside and closed the door behind her, she noticed the small working space. Four desks with computers filled the area, each desk facing into the middle of the room. A fifth desk butted up against the wall had a tilted top and was littered with scraps of paper. That was where the weekly newspaper was pasted together and readied for the printer.

Toward the back of the room, a partition stood, separating what Kathleen guessed to be the bathroom from the office area. A glass door on the right led to an outside deck.

Berens looked up from his computer and smiled at Kathleen. She saw he was dressed in a T-shirt and cutoff jeans. He was barefoot.

"Working on Saturday?" she asked as she settled into a hard chair in front of his desk.

"Oh, I work seven days a week, 18 hours a day." He rubbed his hand through his balding red hair, took off his glasses and cleaned them on the bottom of his shirt. His face was ordinary, but he was filled with nervous energy. A part of his body always seemed to be moving.

"Why?" Kathleen asked, wondering if he had any home life.

"This business is my soul."

Kathleen laughed. "Well, I've known driven journalists before, but never to that extent."

Berens continued to clean his glasses, a hint of his nervousness with her.

"I opened this business six months ago by the skin of my teeth and whatever I could scrape together from relatives. It's been tough because I've been publisher, editor, lead reporter, and advertising manager."

He motioned to the back partition. "I sleep here, I eat here and I dream here. I dream of making the *Chronicle* a real force in this community."

"What about the other paper in town? It's been here for almost 30 years. Isn't that a force in this community?" Kathleen had a slight edge to her voice.

"Oh, it's an OK paper, winning its share of awards. But it has very little of the kind of reporting that I want you to do," he said pointedly, finally putting his glasses on. He looked directly at her.

Kathleen felt a little unnerved by his directness. "What kind of reporting is that? I'm not into sensational journalism—you've obviously read my work or you wouldn't have asked me here. If you think I would be willing to change my professional ethics, you're dead..."

Berens blushed. "Wait a minute, Kathleen, if I can call you that. I didn't mean to offend you. It's just that I'm looking for a different kind of coverage of this town. It's not sensational stories that I'm after, but I am looking for stories that tell how it really is here, not just the glossy public relations crap that comes out of pretty picture magazines showing the police chief grinning with his cronies from the Kiwanis Club. I want the underlying story."

Berens got up from his chair and began pacing back and forth like a caged animal.

"Besides the why of what goes on here, I want to show the diversity of this place. This is not a close-knit community, it's only close for the insiders, those who own and control Sedona.

In truth, it's about as fractured as any community I've ever seen. It's a city of refugees. You know it and I know it because we're refugees here too, looking for our own slice of heaven."

Kathleen interrupted his speech. "Do you think your readers want those kinds of stories?"

Berens was quick to answer. "I don't give a goddamn what my readers want! It's what I want. I want stories about those who come just for the spirituality of this place because of some hokey energy propaganda New Agers pass around. I want stories about the scam artists who make money off of those poor souls trying to find their spirituality. I want stories about the real estate agents intent on selling every goddamn piece of open land, God save their greedy souls, and I want stories about the U.S. Forest Service bureaucracy and the gung-ho environmentalists, particularly an old geezer by the name of John Perkins who is a real pain in everybody's ass.

"You've got one hell of a community to write about Kathleen—each faction fighting for what they desire."

He took a deep breath and continued. "I want the good, the bad and the superb meaninglessness about this place that knocks over everyone with its red rock beauty. I want you to dig into it, smell it, taste it, go climb on Bell Rock and see for yourself if you can touch God."

He stopped pacing, sat back down in his chair and smiled for the first time.

"I want to shake this place up, and I know you have the talent to help me do it. But I want to warn you, I can be a nasty son of a bitch when there are production problems."

Kathleen found herself intrigued by this passionate man. "And you, Jack, where do you fit into the life here?"

"Me? Why I'm a rabid environmentalist who insists on riding a destructive mountain bike everywhere in these red rocks when I have time to leave this goddamn computer. That's how I let off the tension that will probably kill me someday."

Kathleen was silent. She fiddled with her purse handle, thinking. She loved writing articles like Jack described, the in-depth profile story that gives the reader a small, but tell-tale glimpse into the character of the person or place being profiled. She was tired of covering the Phoenix City Council's political dreariness.

"I don't know, Jack." Her voice was uncertain.

"What's there not to know?"

"I like what you would want me to do, although I know you can't pay me the kind of salary I'm already getting at the Republic. But more important, I don't really see any advantage to working in this town. I think you know that I have some bad memories attached to this place."

Jack Berens walked around his desk and leaned back into it, facing Kathleen.

"Look, Kathleen. I know who you were married to. I also can guess what life must have been like as Scott Buckley's wife living among Sedona's wealthy. Those people never knew who you really were before you married Scott. All they knew was that you gave marvelous dinner parties and you could carry on the best of conversations. The next thing they knew is that you left Scott and Sedona, and the impression was that you left with your tail between your legs."

She looked up at him, surprised by his accurate analysis of her previous life. Kathleen stared hard at Jack, trying to discern who he really was.

Funny, she thought. I can't get a read on this guy. She felt inclined to pass up his offer because she sensed he would be difficult to work with.

"Well, if you come back to Sedona to work for me, it will sure as hell give the insiders something to talk about."

She raised a dark eyebrow, waiting. Jack aimed his remark to hit Kathleen's apparent vulnerability.

"It will show you've got guts, Kathleen. It will show that you have the audacity to lift up your tail and piss on them."

Her face hardened for a moment, but she remained silent. Jack Berens took her silence as a positive answer.

"Here, Kathleen," he said, handing her a piece of paper he picked up from his desk. "Here's your first assignment."

MEMO

To: Kathleen Sullivan
From: Jack Berens
Subject: The effect of the new Sedona sewer system.

The city is mandated to construct a new sewer system that will cost millions because Oak Creek, which runs through the city, is being contaminated by the failure of old septic systems. All this political crap has landed on Sedona because Oak Creek has been named a national scenic waterway by the feds.

I want you to interview someone who has been financially pinched by having to pay the $2,100 connection fee. How about one of those old ladies or gents who live in the older mobile homes in Harmony Hills and who don't have a nice word to say about Sedona?

CHAPTER 7

It was late afternoon when Kathleen sat down on the side porch of her small mobile home and took off her glasses. She rubbed the sweat from around her eyes with her shirttail and watched the crew of men in front of her house dig the new city sewer line with a large rock trencher.

The men were knee deep in mud from the downpour that had come before dawn and midmorning. The rain was the normal summer monsoon that sweeps through northern Arizona, bringing clapping thunder and lightning strikes that reverberate along Sedona's rock formations causing hikers and golfers to scurry for cover. The rain had made the street a virtual sea of red, sticky mud.

The day couldn't have turned out worse, Kathleen thought as she watched the construction crew. She felt the tension from the day's move: her arms felt heavy as lead and her right eye ached, deep into the socket, the reason for her removing her contacts and wearing her glasses.

When Kathleen's moving truck had arrived at 7 a.m., the rock trencher just turned the corner of her street and was heading inch by inch toward her front yard like a giant prehistoric monster. As the truck maneuvered around the trencher and came to a halt in front of her house, one of the men from the construction company began yelling at the moving truck's driver.

"Hey, bud! You can't park there. Can't you see we're getting ready to dig the trench in front of that house?"

The moving man, clad in a one-piece jump suit with the logo of his company on the right pocket, looked back at the construction worker as he opened the truck door and climbed out. The other two movers, dressed the same, climbed out on the opposite side of the truck. All three were beefy-looking men.

The truck driver took off his Suns baseball cap and wiped his forehead. "Listen, man, I'm on a tight schedule. I've got to unload this stuff as soon as I can because I'm due in Salt Lake City by tomorrow morning."

The construction worker, filthy because of the mud, shook his head. "Hey, dude, we're on a tight schedule, too. We can't just stop our work while you're parked in front unloading.

You've got to move into the driveway or something."

"Yeah? Well, I guess you can see that I can't get into the driveway. It's too narrow. Got any more brainy suggestions?" the driver said with anger in his voice.

Kathleen heard the yelling and walked out to the driveway to see what was going on. The two men looked like they were going to come to blows.

"Is there some kind of problem?" Kathleen asked the construction worker.

"Yes, there is. Your moving man has parked where we need to dig the trench."

The truck driver turned to Kathleen. "They can't make me move. There's no place else for me to park and get your furniture moved in without it taking hours longer than it should."

The situation appeared to be at an impasse until a pickup truck with mud clear up to the wheel rims drove around the corner and stopped next to the trencher. The driver climbed out, a man Kathleen guessed to be in his mid-fifties looked like the construction foreman. He looked around, sizing up the situation and asked, "What's going on here, Lloyd?"

"Mr. Andrews—we're in the process of finishing this section. Another few hours of work here and we can move the trencher over to the other side of Andante Drive. That would put us nearly back on schedule."

Andrews considered his employee's words for a moment and looked at Kathleen, who was standing at the end of her driveway with a worried look on her face.

"Is there any way your movers could wait while we get this done?" Andrews asked.

"No, way, man!" the mover interjected, repeating his Salt Lake City story.

Andrews rubbed his sweaty forehead, thinking for a long moment. "Well, we're a day behind now, I don't see how a few more hours can hurt us any more than the rain did this morning. It wouldn't be productive at all to move the rock trencher over to Andante while this lady gets moved in, but there's preparation work to be done on Harmony Drive, so send your men over there for the time being, Lloyd."

The construction worker shrugged his shoulders in response. Andrews looked hard at his employee and the man turned on his heel to give orders to the men standing in the street.

Kathleen felt she needed to apologize for her movers. "I'm really sorry about this. I just didn't realize your crew would be working in front of my house today."

"It's not your fault, Miss..."

She extended her hand. "Kathleen Sullivan is my name."

"Richard Andrews," the construction foreman responded. He took her hand in his for a moment, and she could feel the roughness.

"Well, I'm sorry anyway. I know you have a schedule to keep. Thanks for your help. I guess I couldn't have picked a lousier day to move back into this town. I wonder if this is a sign I should have stayed away." She laughed nervously and looked up at the gathering clouds.

Andrews had a rueful look on his face. "I've got a word or two about this place, but it wouldn't help matters any. I'm sorry my company even got the bid for this job. No one expected there would be so much hard rock under the surface. We've had delay after delay."

Andrews took off his hard hat for a moment and ran his hand through his gray hair, which was sticking to the sides of his head from the humidity. He looked straight into her eyes and smiled. His green eyes were friendly.

"I hope your movers can get you in without too much trouble. This mud won't help you much," he said as he turned to get back into the pickup truck.

Despite repeated cleaning of boots, the three moving men still tracked red mud into Kathleen's mobile home. What they thought would take two hours, took longer because her large furniture did not fit well into the small home, forcing them to change arrangements several times.

To top the day off, a midmorning downpour stopped them for forty minutes because her expensive furnishings would have been ruined if they were exposed to the rain.

Several times Richard Andrews drove down the street to check on the movers. Finally at 11 a.m., four hours after the moving van drove in, it pulled out.

Andrew's crew was not far behind, Kathleen noted as she sat resting on the side porch, under her carport. When the rock trencher began digging, the loud grating noise forced Kathleen back into the house. For some inexplicable reason, she hoped Richard Andrews would stop by again, but she could see he was busy directing his crew. She instinctively liked this man. He had a sense of responsibility she appreciated.

Kathleen began unpacking boxes in the small kitchen. Many of them had been in storage since she left Scott. She opened one box, and unwrapped the newspaper, finding a large Orrefors crystal vase. She cleaned it, remembering it was a wedding present, and the many times she filled the vase with roses from the garden she'd planted at Scott's house.

She felt the smoothness of the crystal and the weight of it. It reminded her of the richness of her former surroundings. Here, in this little home, Kathleen was not sure where to place the vase, so she set it down on the sink and began unpacking another box.

The ceramic kitchen canisters needed washing, but when she turned on the kitchen faucet there was a loud thud. After several tries, Kathleen realized no water was coming into the mobile home and her impatience got the best of her.

"Damn it! What's the matter now?"

Just as she was thinking of calling the water company, Kathleen heard a knock at her back door. Richard Andrews stood on the small porch.

He smiled at her and she felt a tingle go down her spine. "Hi...we've hit a water main in the street. You'll be out of water for a while. We've notified the water company...sorry for the inconvenience."

She was flustered by his smile. "I...I appreciate you're notifying me. I wondered what happened to my water. Well, at least I've got water in the kettle."

Not knowing what prompted her to ask, she said to Richard, "Can I offer you a cup of instant coffee or tea?"

She expected him to say he was busy with the crew, but instead he nodded, saying, "Thanks. That would be nice. I need a break."

Richard Andrews eyed the pile of boxes as Kathleen set two cups of steaming coffee on her French cherry wood dining table.

"Sorry about the mess," she apologized.

He took off his hard hat and placed it on the floor before sitting down. "I moved many times in my life when I was with the military. I don't envy you cleaning this up."

He looked around him, noting the rich, French country furnishings in pale pastel colors. The carpet, a holdover from the days when earth tones were popular, did not match her furniture.

Based upon the expensive-looking furnishings, Richard guessed the mobile home must be a change from her former surroundings and he wondered why. She was exquisite, he thought, with loose dark hair and eyes; a woman who belonged in a home that fit the graceful way she carried herself—most certainly not in this cramped place.

He smiled, looking directly at her as he picked up the delicate china coffee cup and noticed the exhaustion in her eyes. When she glanced away from his direct gaze, he realized he made her uncomfortable with his forthrightness.

"Where did you move from?" he asked quietly.

"Phoenix. But I lived there for only a few months. I lived previously in Sedona for twelve years."

He glanced at Capital Butte from her dining room window. "This place must hold something for you, if you've come back a second time."

His blunt fingers carefully maneuvered the delicate cup to his lips. It tasted good and he was bone tired. Kathleen did not respond to his indirect question, so he continued to try to draw her out.

"It's surely beautiful enough to have been carved by the hand of God. I've noticed there seems to be lots of people here who consider this a sacred or spiritual place. Do you?"

Her answer was blunt. "No, Sedona doesn't hold anything spiritual for me. I'm here because of my work, although I know the New Agers consider this a place of spiritual power. I've never quite understood why they flock here to meditate on some rock or other. I really don't understand what it is they think they find. Sedona is striking with its red rock beauty, but I do get terribly tired of the commercialism that sells this place to tourists and New Agers."

"Yes, it seems Sedona does get run over with them," he answered.

Kathleen looked at him in a strange manner and Richard wondered if she thought he was into the New Age philosophies by his question. He knew he certainly didn't look like those aficionados with the clothes of his work—big heavy boots, Levi's, and a short sleeved laundered shirt. And he wore no crystal necklace, a sure sign of the New Age follower.

"Do you live in Sedona?" she asked.

"Well, I do for the time being, but my home is really Phoenix and that's also my company's home base although we bid on jobs all throughout the southwest. The company successfully bid this sewer project, and I'm here only until the job is completed."

"And how long do you think that will be?" There was a hint of disappointment in her voice.

His green eyes took on a hint of worry. "I don't honestly know. It's been a tough job. As I mentioned before, we've had some terrible delays, which has cost the company a great deal of money. No one expected there to be such impenetrable rock. It's taken weeks longer than we estimated."

"If you're behind, how do you make up the time?"

"We work nights with large floodlights and on Saturdays. I know it gets to be quite a grind on everyone—the residents especially—with the noise and the dust and the inconvenience of having streets blocked or torn up. What I don't understand is why so many of these residents are so angry, angry about every little thing. I'm sorry to say that my men have taken some terrible verbal abuse from some of these people...anyway, as I started to say, I haven't been home in weeks."

"I'm sure that must be hard on your family."

Richard rubbed the stubble on his chin, then took his glasses off and cleaned them with a handkerchief he pulled from his pocket. Instead of the coffee perking him up, he felt drained.

"I guess it's hard, but my wife has known lots of years when I was gone because of one military assignment or another, particularly during the Vietnam War. She works and also keeps busy with the grand kids," he said.

There was a knock on the back door. When she opened it, Kathleen's friend, Carrie, stood on the porch.

"Hi, Carrie. Come on in," Kathleen said, surprised to see her.

The two women maneuvered around the boxes leading to the kitchen. Richard got up from the dining room table and put on his hard hat.

After introductions, Richard said, "Thanks for the coffee. I needed a break."

"Thank you for telling me about the water line," Kathleen said as he made his way out the door.

"Well, well, what's this?" Carrie said with a smile after he left. "Not even settled in your house and you've got a man over for coffee."

"Oh, Carrie, it's nothing! He's been very kind to me today. My movers caused a delay for his construction crew. I just offered him a cup of coffee, that's all," she said, angry at herself that she was acting flustered.

"He's a nice looking man, Kathleen. Did he ask you out?" her friend probed hopefully.

"For heaven's sake, Carrie! It was just a cup of coffee! Besides, he's married."

"Really? Well, you have to watch out for those married ones. They look so innocent and then zingo—you fall into bed with them."

"Well, not this old broad! After Scott, I don't need any kind of male involvement. Although I have to say, I am attracted to him. I like the way he looks me directly in the eye. Scott never ever did that; he was so busy dancing around with his pack of lies." Kathleen's voice sounded thin.

"I know...I'm sorry, Kathleen. I didn't mean to bring up such a lousy subject. Anyway, I brought you a home cooked meal. I knew you would be far too tired to cook tonight. It looks like I was right," Carrie said, looking around at the unpacked kitchen.

After Carrie left, Kathleen remembered she needed to get to the post office before it closed. She quickly stuck the chicken casserole in the oven on low heat, grabbed her keys and purse and backed her car out of the driveway into the mud and rubble in the street.

The afternoon had turned hot and muggy. Large billowy clouds gathered in the north, warning of more rain. Traffic on Highway 89A was heavy with cars from California, Minnesota, and Ohio. Tourists were rubbernecking at the spectacular scenery, causing Kathleen to swear at their slow speed.

It was 4 o'clock, a time when most post offices see a lull in business, but not at Sedona's main post office, where many residents rent boxes rather than have mail delivered at home.

Traffic ran heavy there most of the day, particularly when Social Security checks arrived, and drivers continually jockeyed for a parking spot, running the risk of an accident in the overcrowded lot.

She parked at the farthest end of the lot and ran inside, hoping not to come across any of her previous friends. When she was married to Scott, she always looked well-dressed when she stepped out of the house, wearing fashionable casual clothes. Today, her hair hung unbound and she wore a long T-shirt hanging outside of her Levi's.

Her post office box was swollen with forwarded bills, magazines, and an official-looking letter from Maricopa County Superior Court. There was also a letter from Kathleen's attorney, Dan Harris. Kathleen ripped open the letter from the court and found a document informing her that October 1 had been set for the hearing of Scott Buckley's will. She tucked it back in the envelope and opened the letter from her attorney.

"Kathleen: I've been trying to reach you, but your Phoenix telephone number has been disconnected. Your new number in Sedona is not listed, so I'm sending this letter with the hope you have received the court document telling you about the hearing regarding Scott's will on October 1.

"I got an earful the other day from Scott's attorney, Ross Price, while having lunch at the Gold Room. Price was in a talkative mood, apparently working on his third martini. Although he was vague, I have the distinct feeling the Buckley family is going to contest your being named a beneficiary. I need to talk to you as soon as possible. Call me at home."

Kathleen stood for several minutes re-reading Dan's letter. "Goddamn it," she said, jamming the letter back into the envelope. Unconsciously, she rubbed the area of her left clavicle.

"Even in death, the bastard rises up to cause me trouble," she muttered.

CHAPTER 8

Sadie McDaniel
"I Thought This Was Going To Be My Golden Years"
By Kathleen Sullivan
The *Sedona Chronicle*

Sadie McDaniel is verging on 75 years and facing the proverbial wolf at her door.

Sadie, always the realist because she's lived through the Great Depression and the travails of World War II, minces no words, says what she thinks and to hell with the rest of the world.

Regarding that proverbial wolf, Sadie simply wishes it would do what it has to do. Her thinking is: "Get it over with, by God."

Of course, there really is no wolf at Sadie's door. "I'm referring to poverty," Sadie says.

It's been a tough year for Sadie, whose gray hair shows through the red dye that's beginning to fade. She keeps fussing with her hair, a trait she's carried with her since she was a young girl with bright hopes that she would make it to Hollywood someday and become a movie star. The closest she ever got to Hollywood was when she was 18 years old and named Miss Mason City, Iowa. Life never got more exciting for Sadie than that.

After high school, Sadie got a job at the big Armour & Co, meat packing plant; eventually working up to Meat Processing Plant Manager where she inspected meat and meat products and made sure the flow of production was working at a premium level.

"By the early '70s, I was making $17 an hour. I had bought my own home and moved my mom and dad in with me. Everything was great until Valentine's Day, 1975, when to everyone's horror the owners announced the plant would close that summer. Can you imagine, on Valentine's Day they announced that!"

Sadie shakes her head in remembrance. "More than two hundred people were laid off right away. I was lucky…they kept me on until the plant closed in August, and I had a chance to find another job with a meat packing company in Sioux City.

"But it was hard, you know…moving away from the place where I was born. Mom and Dad didn't want to leave. They moved into a small apartment so I could sell the house and relocate. Oh, it was so sad!"

As hard as Sadie tries, a small tear moves slowly down her cheek, but she quickly brushes it away. She squares her shoulders and begins telling her story about a hacking cough that began a year ago.

"It wouldn't go away," Sadie laments, adding that she tried to cure it with a plethora of over-the-counter medicines. After several months of endless hacking, she decided to make an appointment with the visiting county nurse who comes periodically to the Sedona senior citizens center. Her tuberculosis test showed positive.

Despite treatment from the county, Sadie is not sure she will live through this latest disaster. She's not even sure she wants to.

"I'm so damn mad. I caught this TB thing just because I needed some extra money and rented out a room to this kid with a ring in his nose. You know, one of those guys who have moved into Sedona and worship that Indian guru, whatever-his-name-is. Anyway, I thought the kid was always coughing because he smoked too much. Instead the creep gives me TB," Sadie says.

But that's not all the tenant with the ring in his nose gave Sadie. He gave her a hole in her bank account.

Her life savings of $2,208 was taken after she withdrew the money from the bank to pay the $2,100 fee to hook up to the new city sewer system. She withdrew the whole amount because she knew the bank—the one that pretended to be her friend when she moved to Sedona with all her money—would take the remaining $108 in dribbling monthly service fees.

Sadie lives in a run-down mobile home in West Sedona; one side of the porch sags as if it just can't stand up anymore—a little like Sadie. Inside, the cat litter box hasn't been changed in a while, causing a strong smell of cat urine to permeate the place. Gray cat hair sticks to most everything in the mobile home, and the mangy cat hisses at everyone.

She admits she hasn't kept up with her household chores because she hasn't felt well. To make matters worse, the tenant with the ring in his nose also trashed the room he rented.

"Look at this room, would you? I didn't realize people could be such pigs," Sadie moans. She points to the door that is hanging by one hinge, a wall that has been beaten in with a blunt object, and Sadie won't even show the guest bathroom.

Sadie adjusts her eyeglasses that have a crack along the bottom of the right lens, her tongue clicking in disgust.

The deadline for Sadie to connect to the sewer system was three months ago. With every passing day, her fear escalates. She's afraid to call the city and explain to some uncaring bureaucrat why she can't connect to the sewer; she's afraid to call the police to report the kid who took her money because she knows they won't believe a sick, old woman; and she's afraid to open the front door for fear of who will be standing there—a city official handing her a notice to vacate her property. Sadie's little home, as run down as it is, is her only refuge in her retirement

"I moved to Sedona about eight years ago from the Midwest," Sadie says, smoothing her apron with her wrinkled hands. She moves toward the mangy cat, but he hisses at her too. She shrugs.

"My Lord, what a time I've had here! I thought this was going to be my golden years. I came out on one of those senior citizen bus trips and just fell in love with the place. The red rocks are so beautiful, and the weather here seemed so much nicer than Iowa that I decided to sell my home and move to Sedona. But things are higher here than Iowa. I never expected to pay so much for gasoline, for instance. Why it's a full 20 cents a gallon higher than Phoenix! And I have to drive to Cottonwood or Flagstaff just to find a cheap sweat shirt. There's nothing inexpensive in this town!"

Sadie covers her mouth, trying not to cough while she has a guest in her house.

"My savings just whittled down with one thing and another, even though I've been real frugal, mind you! But this sewer thing threw me for a loop. It's the last straw."

Sadie doesn't notice the beauty of the red rocks much anymore. What she sees are the weeds in her little yard that she doesn't have the strength to pull. What she notices is a pile of unpaid bills sitting next to her telephone, which will be disconnected this week for lack of payment.

But Sadie has food. Thanks to the kindness of the Sedona Food Bank, there's sustenance. But the latest food box sits in a corner of the kitchen, unpacked.

Sadie isn't very hungry these days. She's nervous and keeps looking out her dirty front window. She just spends her time waiting for that knock on her door, but she's hoping death will take her first. That would be easier than losing her home, she admits.

Smoothing her apron once more, Sadie coughs, and looks up with a bit of the old twinkle in her eyes. "What a crappy way to go," she cackles, finding some humor in her situation.

Brightening even more, thinking about her troubles with Sedona's new sewer system, she adds, "Yeah, but Sedona is going down the toilet, too. Straight down the toilet! The city doesn't care that this new sewer system has put a lot of old people in a money crunch, not only me. We're all upset about this. I know because it's all the talk at the Senior Center!"

Sadie thinks a bit about what she has just said and then straightens up a bit, sitting taller. That can-do-it attitude from her years as a top-notch meat packer still fuels strength to her soul.

An idea has hit her.

"Why, if that's the case, then I'll get all these old codgers together and we'll fight the city. Like that saying from that movie...you know the one, 'We're madder than hell and not going to take it anymore!'"

She hoots a little, a sound that brings a hiss from the cat. Looking down, she laughs again and tells the cat to shut up, a sly smile on her face.

"Yes, of course, that's what I'll do—fight the city; that's exactly what I'll do!"

CHAPTER 9

The warm summer night smelled of night blooming jasmine, but Philip had more important things on his mind as he hurried up the sidewalk to the Arizona Biltmore. He didn't notice the eclectic architecture of the gracious old resort, or the scores of beautifully dressed people going into the lavishly decorated banquet room set up for the evening's political fund raiser.

Philip was intent on creating a connection with Judge Kenneth Oswald, a man he barely knew above a handshake. Oswald was the Superior Court judge assigned to hear the Buckley probate case. Although Philip knew he could say nothing directly to the judge about the case, he needed to look Oswald straight in the eye and somehow get across to him that there would be rewards if the judge threw Kathleen off the will. Philip knew he could say what he needed to say with tact and diplomacy, but was unsure if Oswald was the type of man who would pick up on the fine nuances of political payback.

The lobby was crowded, but when Philip gave his name at the table outside the banquet room, he was personally escorted to a table directly below the dais, where the Vice President of the United States would make his pitch for funds to keep the Democratic National Committee in the black.

As he settled into his $5,000 seat, Philip felt the rewards of directing a corporation that brought him great wealth and prestige and he had every intention of keeping it that way. Most of the other people at the table were also of the same ilk. Among them was the president of a Fortune 500 technology company based in Arizona, a well-known heart surgeon from the Arizona Heart Institute, two high-powered representatives from the Arizona State Assembly, and place cards on his left showed the names of Judge Oswald and his wife.

Oswald, a distinguished-looking man in his early 60s, instantly recognized Philip when he and his wife were ushered to their seats. The judge was aware of the upcoming Buckley probate case on his docket, and his nervousness was apparent as he cleared his throat while introducing his wife to everyone at the table. A beautiful blond woman, Marion Oswald was obviously twenty years younger than the judge.

On purpose after the introduction, Philip turned to his dinner partner on the right and began chatting, but he could hear Oswald say to his wife, "I think this is some kind of a mistake.

We most definitely don't belong at this table."

Marion squeezed her husband's hand. "Oh, Ken...let's enjoy it while we can! I can't believe we're so close to Vice President Gore. I just hope they don't kick us out of here in the middle of dinner."

A bit later, while the orchestra was quietly playing, Philip turned his attention to the Oswalds.

"I know that I've met you somewhere, but I just can't place it," Philip said.

The judge nodded. "Marion and I met you briefly at the state victory party for the President when he was elected last November."

Philip's face lit up. "Oh, yes, of course! Now I remember. That was one wonderful party, wasn't it?"

The judge nodded and Marion chimed in, "My God, it felt so wonderful to get a Democrat back into the White House!"

Philip leaned forward in a more intimate pose. "Yes, I do agree. I think this country is moving forward again. It's nice to see the Republicans take a back seat for a change." In reality, Philip didn't give a damn about who was in the White House; he believed he knew how to finagle a deal equally with either a Republican or Democrat, depending, of course, on their corruptibility.

The threesome chatted amiably about the hot weather, the baseball season and events in the news. Oswald seemed less nervous as the plates of beef Wellington, asparagus with Hollandaise sauce and hearts of palm salad were served. He gave his wife a playful nudge. "Well, I guess we won't get kicked out of these seats after all."

Marion Oswald looked at her husband with love in her eyes. "This is glorious, Ken. Never in my life have I ever been this close to anyone famous, let alone the Vice President of the United States. He's so handsome and his wife is much prettier than she looks on TV. God, I love her gown! Oh, honey, I don't know what you did to get these seats, but this is so exciting!"

The judge's face lit up under his wife's adoration, but said nothing.

Philip smiled to himself when he heard Marion's remark. The meal was not commensurate with the money he paid to get the Oswalds at his table, but that was peanuts compared to what he would lose if Kathleen received part of the estate and decided to fight the land trade.

The dessert was particularly delectable, a white chocolate torte with raspberry sauce, and then the tables were quickly cleared and the speeches began. Philip half listened, his mind on the matter at hand. When the politicking finished and the applause died down, Vice President Gore walked off the dais and headed toward Philip's table, personally thanking a select few for their donation to the party. As he came to Philip, he said, "Nice to see you again, Philip. May I extend my condolence on the death of your brother?" When Philip nodded, Gore added, "Let me know the next time you're in Washington. I'd like you to drop by my office."

Oswald and his wife sat in their seats, dumbstruck by the closeness of the Vice President, and Philip saw the look on their faces. In a bold move, he placed his hand on Oswald's shoulder. "Mr. Vice President, I would like you to meet one of this state's most distinguished judges, Superior Court Judge Kenneth Oswald and his lovely wife, Marion."

The Vice President graciously leaned over and extended his hand to the judge and nodded to his wife. "It's nice to see representation from the judiciary here tonight. I'm very pleased to meet you both."

Later, as others at the table began to move toward the dance floor, Marion excused herself to go to the ladies room. When she left, an awkward silence hung between Philip and the judge. Finally, Oswald turned to Philip. "Thank you for that introduction to the Vice President. I'm not sure I deserved your compliment, but my wife is on cloud nine."

Philip looked directly at Kenneth Oswald who was taking a sip from his glass of wine. "Ken, I believe in getting directly to the point. I understand there will soon be an opening on the Federal court for this district. I have connections, Ken...you most certainly saw that just now. Why don't you let me make more happy evenings for you and your lovely wife?"

The judge choked a little on his drink and stammered, "I...I'm not sure I understand."

Philip turned slightly and saw that Marion was making her way back across the banquet room. Now was the time to move in for the kill. His voice was as smooth as glass.

"Oh, I think you do understand, Ken, but there's no need to say anything about pressing court cases coming up on your docket. You saw how much Marion loved this evening and I'm sure you want to continue giving her the good life—all you have to do is reach out and grab it. It wouldn't take much for me to get you the federal appointment, Ken, not much at all."

Judge Kenneth Oswald sat mute, the terse look on his face showed he understood. A long moment passed, and then he looked over at Philip and silently nodded his head. At that moment, Marion reached the table, barely able to contain her news. "My God, Ken! I just bumped into Barbra Streisand in the bathroom! She was hobnobbing with Tipper Gore!"

As she sat down, Philip got up gracefully from the table and shook hands with the judge whose color was a bit ashen. "I have an urgent phone call to make to Washington, D.C. tomorrow morning, so I must leave a bit prematurely. I have enjoyed your company and I sincerely hope to visit with you again."

After Philip left, Oswald was quiet for a while and then he took his wife's hand in his and kissed it. "I love you, Marion. You are what keeps me young and alive in a stilted legal world.

I would do anything to keep you as happy as you are tonight."

She laughed gaily and gave him a playful kiss on the lips. "My goodness, Judge! One would think you were trying to get me into bed. Oh, well...I suppose there's got to be some payback for such a divine evening."

Chapter 10

MEMO

To: Kathleen Sullivan
From: Jack Berens
Subject: Jeep Tour Driver

The tourist dollar is what makes Sedona tick and fills the coffers of city hall.
How about talking to one of those over-dressed costumed Jeep tour drivers?
What's it like to give the same spiel hour after hour, day after day? I want
some color in this, Kathleen, down to the bumps in the road.

Troy Jenkins
Still Playing Cowboy
By Kathleen Sullivan
The *Sedona Chronicle*

Troy Jenkins straps on his loaded six-shooter, puts on his black cowboy hat, and then buttons his black vest, dusting off a few flakes of dandruff from his long blond hair tied back in a ponytail.

"I always played cowboy when I was a kid. Now I get to play cowboy as an adult. On cold days, I usually wear one of those long duster coats. You know, the kind that Clint Eastwood wore in his last cowboy movie."

As he heads out the side door of the small house he rents with two other men, Troy takes out his wallet and looks inside.

"Hmm...only $25 until payday. I'm gonna have to be real good today," he says, referring to the tips he receives from his passengers.

As he drives into Uptown Sedona in his beat-up Plymouth, Jenkins scans the number of tourists waiting in front of the Jeep tour company he works for. Based upon the crowd, Troy judges It's going to be a busy day.

After checking in with the tour office, Troy gathers his flock. There are three elderly people, a husband and wife from San Diego and a man from Germany. The last couple—in their mid-thirties—are from Dallas. They have two kids, about ten and twelve.

"Howdy, I'm Troy and I'm your driver today. It's my great pleasure to introduce you to the beauty of the red rocks," Troy says, eyeing them carefully, sizing the group up for tips.

Judging from past experience, Troy confidentially says he might get a good tip from the San Diego couple, but the man from Germany will probably only give him about $2. Most Europeans are fairly skimpy with their tips, he adds.

As for the couple from Texas, his tip will depend on whether or not they are charging everything. "If so, I'm tough s... out of luck."

Addressing his group, Troy says, "You've picked an off-road tour into the area near Vultee Arch. Although the road is rough, I've driven rougher, but I'll try to make it as smooth as possible for your comfort. I haven't lost any tourists yet," he laughs, patting the head of the 10-year-old boy who is eyeing Troy's gun.

"Hey, man! Is that real?" the kid says, lightly touching the handle.

"Yes, it is, son. And it's loaded, just in case we come across some kind of varmint." Moving away from the kid, he says, "I'd appreciate it if you'd not touch the gun."

"Varmint? What kind of a varmint could be out here?" asks the boy's mother, a touch of fear in her Texas drawl, ignoring the fact that her son touched the Jeep driver's gun.

"Well, ma'am, Arizona is noted for her rattlesnakes. I've seen enough to make my hair the color blond that it is. We've also got a few coyotes, javelina, and a hairy tarantula or two."

"Do you shoot them when you see them?" she asks, holding onto her daughter's arm as if a rattlesnake were coiled nearby.

"Not the rattlesnakes, ma'am, only the tarantulas," Troy says with a grin. The woman shakes her head in disgust. She doesn't appreciate his wry Arizona humor.

Troy stiffens, sensing this tour might be a little tough. He loads the group into the Jeep and steps in himself, checking his gun belt as he swings into the driver's seat.

"Ready? Hope you all have film for your cameras. I'm going to be stopping at some spectacular spots, and I know you'll want to take photos. I've just got to warn you about one thing. The dust. It may get in your eyes and your mouth, but we don't need anyone taking Sedona's dust home with them, so we'll charge you by the ounce unless you shake yourself off when we get back!"

Everyone chuckles, and Troy smiles as he takes off down Highway 89A toward West Sedona, pointing out some of the highlights of the rock formations.

"Over to the left there lies Snoopy on his back. See him? And if you look real careful, there's Woodstock over there perched on the top of that mountain above Snoopy."

Everyone murmurs as they locate the two cartoon characters carved in stone by nature herself.

"Isn't this a spectacular place? I say a prayer every day, giving thanks that I live and work here. I also say a prayer that some dumb driver doesn't stop dead in front of me on this crazy highway." Troy checks his speed, keeping an eye out for the Sedona police.

"Where do you hail from?" the man from San Diego asks Troy.

"Where everybody hails from around here—Los Angeles, which isn't the city of Angels anymore," he chuckles again at his own joke.

"How long you been doing this?" the man asks.

"Oh, about two years. Every day I get to see this beauty and tell you folks about it."

"God, you are lucky at that," agrees the man, looking at the red formations standing against the bright blue sky.

Moving south along the highway, Troy points out Coffee Pot Rock. "See that, over there? That's been named Coffee Pot Rock. Sure looks like one doesn't it? If any of you happen to remember the old John Wayne movie, *Angel and the Badman*, you can see Coffee Pot Rock as clear as daylight in a lot of the background shots."

"This is pretty, but not near so pretty as some of our Rio Grande country," the Texas woman drawls to her husband.

Trying to keep his voice low, he answers, "Well, it's different, I'll give Arizona that much. I just hope this ride is worth the money; this really doesn't fit into our budget. We'll have to eat at a fast food restaurant for dinner to cut down on today's expenses."

Further down the highway, Troy turns at Dry Creek Road.

"Now, there's Chimney Rock and way over there to the left is Cock's Comb," he points out the two formations. After a bit, he pulls the Jeep over to the side of the road and parks.

"There's a Lizard Head on one of these buttes. Can anyone find him?"

The 12-year-old girl whines to her mother, "God, this is dumb. When are we going shopping? I don't want to look for funny rock formations!"

"Hush up, Diedre! Your father paid a lot of money for this Jeep ride. It's supposed to be the thing to do in Sedona."

Troy looks around and lays an eye on the girl.

"Red rocks get a little boring when there's so many interesting shops in Uptown to go through, I know. But I think you'll learn something as we go on our trip today that you can take back to school with you. I know it's hard to imagine, but geologists say that between 320 to 255 million years ago—over a period of 65 million years—the sand that makes up the red rocks you see today was first deposited. At the beginning of that period, Sedona was beach-front property."

The girl suddenly perks up. "Ah, you got to be kidding."

"Nope. Sedona was perched on the edge of a tropical coral sea. About 267 million years ago, the sea began to retreat and Sedona was covered with enormous reddish sand dunes. Then, over millions of years, the red rocks were formed. The red color comes from a combination of iron oxide and water."

"How'd they happen to name the town Sedona," one of the passengers asks.

"As the story goes, Sedona and Carl Schnebly settled here in 1901 and ran a small store, hotel, and post office. Carl originally submitted the name of Oak Creek Crossing and Schnebly Station to the Postmaster in Washington D.C., but the names were rejected because they were too many words for the cancellation stamp. Instead, Carl submitted the name of his wife."

Troy moves the Jeep back onto Dry Creek Road and continues his talk about the area, pointing out the juniper and pinon pines, manzanita, mesquite, and the various wildflowers peeking through brush alongside the road.

At the top of a hill, Troy again pulls over. There's a murmur among the group because of the view.

"I've got to say it folks, this is probably the most spectacular view of Sedona. Lots of commercials are filmed right at this spot because there's no hint of civilization here, no telephone lines or houses in the background."

At another photo stop, everyone scrambles out of the Jeep except Troy and the couple from San Diego. The man leans over to Troy. "Do you guys make a pretty good living driving people around? I notice the sign on the dashboard says tips are welcome. If you depend on tips, life can be a little rough."

"The living we make probably wouldn't satisfy a lot of people, but I'm alone and really have no one that I have to support but myself." Troy answers in a pleasant tone, but shifts uneasily in his seat.

As the others return to the vehicle, the driver holds the front passenger seat back so they can climb into the rear. Once again, the boy brushes past him, touching the gun handle. Troy frowns but says nothing.

Alex gives Troy a flip of his middle finger as he clambers back to his seat, unseen by his parents. Troy walks around the Jeep, a deep frown burrowed into his face, and climbs in, only to find the engine won't turn over. Muttering to himself, Troy gets out again, pulls up the hood, looking for the problem, forgetting his anger for the moment.

"Would you mind getting into the driver's seat and turning on the engine while I tinker here with the battery?" Troy asks the boy's father.

The boy climbs out as his father attempts to start the vehicle. Acting interested in the stalled Jeep, he moves behind Troy as he jiggles the battery cable. The engine starts and as it does, Alex sees another chance to touch the gun.

Aware of the boy's trick, Troy wheels to face the kid, losing his temper, yelling, "I told you not to touch it!"

Startled, the boy jumps back and trips over a rock, lands on his back and starts to cry. Alarmed, the father jumps out of the vehicle and runs to his son, pulling him up off the red dirt. "Alex are you all right?"

The boy, sensing his moment, continues to wail.

The father begins yelling at Troy. "What have you done to him? How dare you yell at my son like that! You'll pay for this, you stupid fake cowboy! What the hell are you doing wearing a real gun anyway?"

"In Arizona, it's legal to wear a gun in a holster," Troy says in a low, angry tone, facing the father. "Your son has been bugging me since we started this trip. I think you should be yelling at him instead of yelling at me because he's touched the gun three times when I told him not to—and not to mention that he flipped me the bird when you weren't looking! Some kid you raised there, mister."

"You'll pay for this," the father shouts again, taking his son by the arm and dragging him back into the Jeep, still whimpering.

Troy shakes his head. If he expected a tip from this ride, he knows there won't be any. He brushes the red dust off his hat and jams it back onto his head.

"Oh, well," he says, loud enough so everyone in the Jeep can hear. "I drive people from all over the world to see these red rocks, and I always wondered where the majority of idiots come from. Now I know for sure. They're from Texas."

CHAPTER 11

The back of Kathleen's neck ached, enough that she stood up from her computer and stretched her arms and back, doing a breast stroke in midair.

"I must be getting old," She said. "I remember when I covered some of the national election campaigns, and I worked twelve to fourteen hours a day. Now I'm beat after a day of tagging along after that Jeep tour guide."

Lauren Winters, the new ad manager of the *Sedona Chronicle* nodded her head in agreement. "I know what you mean. I'm beat after dealing with the business people in this town. They're enough to drive me crazy."

It was nearing lunch time and the small office was empty except for the two women.

"Do you have a hard time selling ads?" Kathleen asked.

"The problem here is too many publications. I had one businessman tell me with disgust that I was the fifth ad person in his shop that morning."

Lauren was designing ads on her computer screen as she spoke. She was a small woman in her early thirties with long, black hair worn straight. Her eyeglasses were wire rimmed and she wore her dresses either long and loose or tight and short. She usually wore black high topped boots with lace-trimmed stockings.

"There's the regular community newspaper which has been in town for over 30 years," Lauren continued. "Most business people advertise with it because of its longevity, and it has a strong readership in the area. Then there are alternative newspapers, one that's humorous, one that touts the old west, and one involved with the New Age. There are also a couple of magazines and several newspapers from out of town that want a piece of Sedona's action."

Lauren's comment prompted Kathleen to ask how the ad manager promoted the *Chronicle* over other publications.

"I have a good selling background with small newspapers in the Los Angeles area. I've learned that readers want local news, particularly the kind of personal profile stories you're writing. The *Chronicle* is better doing that than other publications here, and that's the angle I promote. I've managed to get some good ad accounts, but I've got to get more if this paper is going to survive."

God, I would hate to see this operation go under, Kathleen thought. A small prickle of fear touched her as she thought about the future. Everything seemed so uncertain in her life, even this job.

"Do you like the kind of writing you're doing?" Lauren asked Kathleen as she put the finishing touches on an ad and printed it out.

"It's different than the ordinary feature stories I've done because I spend more time with the person I'm writing about. But, yes I do like it. It's fun to climb into someone's life, if only for a day or two. Jack was right. There are lots of good stories to write about in Sedona."

Lauren looked at her watch. "Hey, it's lunch time, Kathleen. Let's lock the door and go out to eat on the deck."

At that moment, the door opened. A short, gray-haired older woman walked in.

"Excuse me, but I'm looking for a shop that gives a deal on sweatshirts. Forty bucks for a sweatshirt with Sedona printed on it is outrageous. Can you tell me where to find one?"

The woman spoke with a New York accent.

Kathleen, irritated at the woman's intrusion, curtly answered her. "This is a newspaper office. I really don't know where to get a good deal on a sweatshirt unless you go to Flagstaff to the large mall."

"Oh, well, I'm on a tour bus and can't get to Flagstaff," the old woman said, banging the door shut. Kathleen raced to lock it.

"Don't they ever read a sign?" Kathleen asked. "I hate this office being located in the middle of Uptown. Some of these people visiting Sedona are a pain in the ass."

Lauren laughed. "Now, now! They're Sedona's bread and butter. Just listen to the chamber of commerce."

"I know this is a beautiful place, but these people get nuts when they see the red rocks," Kathleen said. "I couldn't believe what I saw the other day as I was driving toward West Sedona, just before the turnoff from Uptown toward the Village of Oak Creek. As I came around the curve, there was this young woman in a turquoise convertible stopped dead in the middle of the left lane taking a photograph. I mean in the middle of the street!"

"Yeah, I know what you mean. The other evening my friends and I went to mediate at the prayer circle on Schnebly Hill Road and there were these young people throwing rocks from the prayer circle over the edge of the mesa! When we asked them what they were doing, they said they were a Christian youth group from Phoenix and they were getting rid of the prayer circles because they're devil worship."

Kathleen looked over at Lauren. "I didn't realize you're into the New Age."

Lauren pulled her lunch out of a desk drawer. "Well, I guess you have a right to be surprised. I don't wear the usual garb, at least not when I'm working. But I definitely am a follower of the New Age."

Kathleen realized her voice sounded judgmental and tried to soften her remark as she retrieved her lunch from the small refrigerator at the back of the office. "I really don't know anything about the New Age. I guess that's surprising for my having lived in Sedona so long."

They walked out to a small patio attached to the back of the building, and it was as if they were transported to another milieu the moment they closed the door. No tourists or cars were visible from the patio, just cottonwood trees growing all the way to the banks of Oak Creek below. The pleasant, damp smell of the creek wafted up to them on the deck. Male cicadas could be heard from the tops of the cottonwood trees, calling loudly for a potential mate.

Kathleen took in a deep breath. "I smell autumn, somehow, even though it's only August. I love this time of the year. There's something very special about it, like an awakening, an expectancy."

She took out her ham sandwich and began to eat. "Tell me what the New Age means. If I'm going to cover this town, I guess I better learn something about it."

Lauren opened up her low-fat yogurt and mixed fruit into the thickened liquid.

"Well, we're people from all walks of life, from hairdressers to engineers to UFO investigators. The New Age isn't a new religion, although fundamentalist Christians accuse us of being one. It's really a philosophy, a way of living. We don't have a chosen hierarchy or rituals. We don't want to convert the world. We have our own way of thinking and we're not street preachers. You can take full exception to what I say. It's not my job to force my philosophy on you."

Kathleen chewed on her sandwich. "Well, then, tell me what your philosophy is,"

"Well, we're people who take conscious responsibility for our own problems. We create our own reality. We're people who see problems as lessons. We believe there are no mistakes in this life, only lessons to be learned from those mistakes."

Kathleen nodded. "OK, now I understand better what New Agers mean when they refer to a certain problem and say this is a lesson they have to learn."

"That's right," Lauren said. "We believe we can only change our own thinking, not anyone else's. Our philosophy is that in order to change someone else, change yourself. I can only change myself and change the world by changing myself."

She looked at Kathleen. "Do you understand what I just said?"

Kathleen found the conversation fascinating. "Yes, a little. Tell me more."

Lauren ate slowly, thinking about her comments. "We're people who choose our own path other than man's written dogma. First we have a responsibility to ourselves, then we accept the responsibility to others."

Kathleen considered Lauren's last comment. "That differs greatly from Christian philosophy, which says that man's first responsibility is to God."

Lauren took a small spoonful of yogurt, continuing. "We're a people who honor your right to your own path. You have a right to feel or believe as you feel."

"Are you saying that New Agers don't hold anything against those of us who believe in Jesus Christ as the son of God?"

"That's right."

"But Christians believe you're wrong in your thinking."

"That's because the New Age has no allegiance to any one master, as the Christians have. We learn from many masters, like Christ, Buddha, Vishnu, and others in the quest of God," Lauren said. "People don't have to be right, except for themselves. That's what spirituality is about—doing what's good for you."

Kathleen laughed. "Boy, that's sure different than what I learned in my catechism classes. Doing for God and others first is how I was brought up. Doing for myself always came last."

"Maybe you need to do for yourself for a change," Lauren suggested.

Kathleen was thoughtful for a moment. "Oh, I tried that! I finally got up enough guts to leave my husband. I did for myself and in the process, I committed a mortal sin in the eyes of my church."

"That must be very hard to deal with," Lauren said. "For us, there are no sins, only lessons. We believe that people gain strength from the universe by going within to find themselves and learning from those lessons. Go into the silence and discover yourself and have the light shining out."

"What do you mean the light shining out?"

"We believe that each person has a part of God within him—our Godself." Lauren finished off her yogurt and bit into a plum.

"Is that why so many people who are into the New Age meditate? To discover their Godself?"

"Yes."

"Why here, why Sedona? Because it's so beautiful?"

"That may have something to do with it. But there are certain areas of Sedona that have been scientifically proven to have high energy levels. We call them vortexes—like at Bell Rock or Boynton Canyon. Going to those areas enhance the meditation process. That's why we wear crystals around our necks. We believe it increases our ability to connect to the universe and the part of each of us that is God."

Kathleen threw pieces of bread crust back into her lunch sack. She searched for her banana and began pealing it back. "Boy, I sure have a lot to learn. Tell me, what do you mean when you talk about dark energy?"

"It's in reference to yin and yang, dark and light, opposites of everything, including man and woman, good and bad. Those are natural forces in the universe. Rather than saying its Satan, or the devil, we don't have the devil to blame like Christians do. Man himself creates the evil in the world, and that includes organized religion."

Kathleen eyed her co-worker. She admired Lauren's spunk, although Kathleen knew she could never personally embrace the New Age philosophy. Catholicism was too ingrained in her soul for her to consider any other kind of spiritual outlook, although she felt respect for those who believed differently than she did.

"Well, Lauren, in a word just what is the New Age?" Kathleen asked, knowing she was probing a soft spot. What she hoped for was an honest answer, not New Age psychobabble.

She raised her eyebrows and smiled when Lauren flipped out her answer.

"It's a journey toward the love of God."

CHAPTER 12

Jack Berens yanked open the door to the patio.

"What are both of you doing out here?" he asked, his voice hard.

"We're eating lunch," Kathleen answered. His angry tone caught her off guard.

"Listen. I'm trying to run a business. What makes you think you can just lock the front door and go sunning on the deck? There may be a customer who wants to place an ad during lunch hour."

Kathleen flushed a little. "Sorry, I didn't consider that. I locked the door because I get tired of answering questions from tourists who wander into the office."

"Has it ever occurred to you that they may want to buy a paper?" he demanded.

Kathleen looked at him for a moment, took a deep breath and decided to confront his anger head on.

"Look, Jack. You didn't hire me to answer questions from tourists or sell them a copy of the newspaper. That's not my job. If you have a problem with what my job is, then let's discuss that. As far as I'm concerned, I'm a newspaper reporter, not a visitor center information specialist. I suggest you hire someone for those chores."

"What do you suggest I pay them with—considering what I pay you?" he spit out.

"That's really not my concern, Jack. I'm not the publisher of the paper, you are."

Jack Berens had been out of the office all morning. Before he left, he informed Kathleen and Lauren he had a social event to attend at L'Auberge de Sedona, the luxury resort hidden beside Oak Creek, yet just a few hundred yards from the hustle and bustle of Uptown Sedona. The resort's lush ambiance reminded Kathleen of the French wine country. She felt a yank on her heartstrings when she heard Jack was going there for lunch, remembering that Scott proposed to her at the resort while they were having cocktails by the creek amid the quacking ducks and the glorious spring flowers.

She gathered her paper sack and walked back into the office. Jack's actions also reminded her of Scott. In fact, he reminded her a little too much of Scott, particularly when her husband was drunk.

She went to her desk and looked over at him. He came in from the patio and was undoing his tie, sweating a little from the heat, his glasses sliding down his nose with the moisture. She threw her sack in the wastebasket with a resounding thump and walked over to him. Better to face him now than later, she thought. If the last episode with Scott had taught her anything, it was that she should not remain silent and let the situation fester.

"You didn't answer me, Jack. Do you want to discuss my job description with me?"

He looked up at her as he yanked at his tie. "Naw. My problem is that I happen to believe that on a small paper, everybody does everything they can to get the paper out, including answering questions from some dumb tourist."

He took off his glasses and began wiping them with a hanky from his pants pocket. "You're a prima donna, Kathleen. I knew that when I hired you, but you're damn good at what you do and the paper shows it. I've gotten plenty of comments about your story on Sadie McDaniels. Some people in town want to help the old woman. And the story on the Jeep tour driver has angered lots of Texans who moved here—damn if they aren't a protective bunch! But that's OK. I told you I wanted to rile this town, and you're doing it! Just do me a favor and take turns on your lunch hour with Lauren so the office isn't closed, huh?"

Kathleen felt the sting of his remark. She also got a whiff of his whiskey-tainted breath. Before she could react, he handed her a legal notice that came into the office with the mail.

"Here, Kathleen, take a look at this. It appears the Forest Service is considering trading a hundred acres of its land near Edgarville for Buckley land in the canyon."

Kathleen read the notice. She knew it meant the beginning of a long process between the Buckleys and the federal agency. There would be public hearings, environmental reports, recommendations from higher ups in the Forest Service. Even after that process, residents in Edgarville could appeal the decision if the Forest Service approved the trade.

"I knew this was coming. It's been in the works for some time." She handed the public notice back to Jack.

"I want a story on it, Kathleen."

Kathleen winced. "You know I can't do that, Jack. I'm involved in this land trade. As a beneficiary of Scott's will, I own part of that land that will be traded. It's a conflict of interest for me to report on the story."

His voice turned nasty. "Well, I don't buy that crap about conflict of interest. Only big-time newspapers get into that ethics stuff. I just want a story about the feelings of the people in Edgarville who thought they bought next to open space, junipers and a cottontail or two. How do they feel about the possibility of a big time development next to their property?"

He continued. "Besides, I hear people out there are a little more independent minded—they're damned upset about that religious group killed by government agents in Waco, Texas.

The land trade ought to rile them even more—they're good Arizona red necks. You should be able to get some good quotes."

She gave Jack a blank look. "What are you talking about?"

"You know, that religious sect, the Branch Davidians. They were burned out in that farm compound. It was a standoff with the FBI, and it happened sometime in April."

When he heard no response from Kathleen, he continued. "You're a news reporter, Kathleen, don't you keep up with this stuff? The government is investigating the incident, but most people believe the report on the siege will be a whitewash. People are beginning to form militias because they're afraid our new liberal president is moving in the direction of gun control—taking away their rights, particularly their right to own guns." There was a note of exasperation in his voice.

"In April? I'm sorry, Jack, but Scott died in April, at Easter," she tried to explain. "I wasn't aware of much that was going on in the world then. I guess I'm still kind of out of it."

He shook his head, as if to dismiss her, but she continued to press about the land trade story being a conflict for her.

"Look, Jack. People around here know I'm a Buckley. What are they going to say if I write that story?"

"You let me worry about that. It seems to me you just made a point of that. I'm the publisher, remember. I'll take the heat."

He rolled his tie into a ball and threw it across the room, a gesture of impatience toward her. It hit the screen that hid his bed, and landed in a rumpled heap. Kathleen guessed it would remain there for a week unless she or Lauren picked it up.

She moved to her desk and tried to gather her thoughts. Despite her resolve to confront problems head on, Kathleen detested such situations and tried to soothe her hurt pride by remembering Jack told her he could be nasty. Kathleen was angry at herself for not paying attention to that revealing comment when he hired her. She noticed Jack was busy pounding out something on his computer. After a few moments, he walked over to the laser printer, picked up the sheet of paper that popped out of it, and dropped it nonchalantly on her desk.

She cringed. It was another one of Jack's goddamn memos. We're in the business of communicating and this guy gives me a memo when I sit six feet across the room from him, she thought, shaking her head in disgust.

MEMO

To: Kathleen Sullivan
From: Jack Berens
Subject: Residents of Edgarville

There's a small community south of Sedona's city limits called Edgarville, where land prices aren't so expensive and the city's picky code enforcement officer can't jump their ass because of a pile of junk in their front yard. I hear these people are unhappy about the proposed Forest Service land trade of a hundred acres that sits adjacent to their community. These people are individualistic, hate the government, and want to be left alone. It would be a perfect story for a former Buckley to cover.

CHAPTER 13

Edgarville
"I Can't Even Imagine a Big Development Next to Me"
By Kathleen Sullivan
The *Sedona Chronicle*

Myron White scratches his scraggly beard and looks out across his vegetable garden toward the open land that belongs to the U.S. Forest Service.

"I've been living here a long time, before most of these other folks came here. I can't even imagine having a big development next to me." He spits a chaw of tobacco over his porch railing, aiming at a weed.

Myron hails from Oklahoma. When the horrors of the Dust Bowl hit his family back in the days of the Great Depression, they headed west. After picking fruit in California for several seasons, the White family eventually settled in Arizona' Myron's father came down with a lung disease, and he lived to 90 with the aid of Arizona's dry climate. Myron's now verging on 80 and he's feisty. He likes to carry his shotgun with him wherever he goes, just in case, he explains, a varmint might appear in his path. With a toothy grin, he explains that might not always be a rattlesnake.

"I don't understand nothin' about this land trade business. It's all a big surprise to me. But, I'll tell you this—anyone, particular anyone looking like they're a fed comin' 'round my property will see a shotgun in his face!" He moves the topic handily from the proposed land trade near Edgarville to a topic that angers him even more—Waco, Texas.

"Me and my friends, we got their number! They think they can just go out and kill those folks in Waco! Well, they've taken a little too much power into their hands. It's time we god-fearin' Constitution-lovin' Americans take this country back from the bureaucrats. And that includes the damn Forest Service! We've had a meetin' or two, we have, and we're thinkin' about forming our own militia! We are, by God!"

Myron isn't alone. Other neighbors, Gene and Mary Blevins, a retired couple who moved to Arizona to get away from Minnesota's cold winters, saw the public notice in local newspapers about the proposed land trade. They're confused and concerned.

Gene Blevins doesn't mind stating his views. "This is our home. We moved out here to get away from people, to feel the beauty of the land. This land trade will ruin all that. The Forest Service shouldn't be allowed to trade land. But it appears that just because the rich Buckley family is involved, the government is willing to change our way of living. Rich people in this country always get what they want. What about us common folk?"

The Buckley Corporation, an Arizona company headed by Philip Buckley, has proposed the swap of ten acres of land along Oak Creek owned by the late Scott Buckley with a hundred acres of forest land adjacent to Edgarville.

Forest Service officials say land swaps are important management tools. Because of cutbacks in the federal budget, the U.S. Forest Service views land swaps as the only way to obtain important property containing dwindling habitats.

The Buckley property contains a valuable riparian habitat along Oak Creek that the agency has wanted for many years, according to a Forest Service spokesperson. The Forest Service does not consider the hundred acres it owns near Edgarville to be an asset because of the proximity of the land to the Edgarville community.

Another resident of Edgarville, Otis Harrisburg, built his home with his own hands about 30 years ago. He believes the land exchange will change everything in his beloved community.

"I'm madder than hell. I just can't believe this. Mark my words, Buckley will put in a paved road and build expensive houses with pools and spas out here! I can just imagine what those people are going to think about our horse flies and the cock crowing at 5 a.m.! They'll want everything nice and neat, and there goes our wonderful little rural community because they'll run and complain to the county to get this all changed."

He laughs, but there is a touch of bitterness in his mirth. "I'm just waiting for those sons of—those feds—to show up and tell me they're trading this beautiful land, and some pricey development is coming in next to me. They'll think a thing or two when I get through with them!"

Harrisburg puts his two hands up near the front of his bearded face, pretending he has a bead on a federal agent. He makes a noise like a bullet flying through space.

"Gotcha!" he says with glee.

Most of the residences in the area are older mobile homes. Recent property owners have built larger modern houses on their acreage where fruit trees and vegetable gardens abound along with scampering children and barking dogs that frolic in the community's dirt road.

Members of the local Sierra Club and Audubon Society have also expressed concern about the proposed land trade, saying bird and wildlife habitats on the Forest Service land adjacent to Edgarville will be disturbed by development.

Anne Brooks, president of the local Sierra Club, expresses amazement at the very thought of a land exchange where the Forest Service would gain only ten acres while giving up one hundred.

"Hey, I know how important that habitat is along Oak Creek! We've been hoping the Forest Service would just plunk down the money and buy the property. Instead they go for a land exchange where they acquire only

10 percent of the land they're giving up. I don't call that a bargain for the American taxpayer, even if it is a valuable habitat."

Philip Buckley, executor for the estate of Scott Buckley, could not be reached for comment. No information currently is available regarding what plans are being made for the property after the exchange is completed.

Forest Service officials estimate the land exchange process could take approximately 18 months.

CHAPTER 14

A freak tropical storm off the Mexican coast blew north and rattled Northern Arizona's normally dry September weather with thunderstorms and flash flood warnings.

Kathleen stood at her kitchen window and watched the driving rain run off her carport, coming down so hard it splashed out of the rain gutters rather than running out the down spouts.

The weather depressed her, bringing on a loneliness that clawed at her soul. In six weeks, she would be facing her 46th birthday. She didn't have much to show for those years, she thought. A failed marriage, no children, and a job she was beginning to worry about.

She didn't like working for a publisher who lacked journalistic ethics. Although she often saw a lack of ethics in some of her colleagues when they had a personal interest in a story that had never been Kathleen's way.

In all her years as a journalist, she never wrote a story where she was personally involved. Since the story about the Edgarville residents, she grew more disgusted with herself for not standing up to Jack.

Damn it, why didn't I just tell him I wouldn't do it, she kept saying to herself. Yet she knew the answer deep within her. She came back to Sedona to prove that she wasn't afraid of the town or the people in it, and that included reporting on the Buckleys and their political maneuvering.

She moved away from the window and began unpacking another box. More than two months had passed since she moved into her mobile home and she still wasn't completely unpacked.

Today, she hoped she could get her china cabinet finished. She was tired of seeing the boxes stacked in the corner of the dining room.

For company, she turned on a local radio station. The broadcaster broke into the music, announcing a flash flood watch for Northern Arizona, warning residents not to travel unless necessary and to stay away from low lying areas.

About an hour later, she opened the back door that led to the carport. As she dragged the empty boxes out, she saw water building up in her driveway, moving toward the foundation of her mobile home. Kathleen dropped the boxes and ran to the edge of the carport.

She could see the sewer construction work had blocked a nearby drainage ditch and the flow of water was sweeping down her driveway instead.

She raced into the house, grabbed her rubber boots and a raincoat and ran to her storage shed where she found a shovel, then began digging into the side of the driveway, throwing shovels of dirt toward the middle in an attempt to build some sort of a makeshift dike that would stop the buildup of water, but the reddish-colored stream moved around the pile she made, still heading toward her home.

At the same time, crews from the sewer construction company began checking streets in the Harmony Hills area because of the heavy rainstorm and found a clogged drainage ditch on Harmony Drive. Water was beginning to inundate the Sedona Adult Community Center.

Richard Andrews shouted to his construction crew. "You guys continue working here until this situation is under control. I'm going to check other streets."

He drove slowly through the heavy rain, looking for any area showing rising water. He turned right down a side street where everything seemed to be fine, but as he turned again, he saw a woman in a red raincoat standing in a driveway filled with water.

Richard jumped out of his truck and grabbed his shovel. She yelled at him, "It's coming toward the house! I don't know how to stop it!"

He recognized her as the woman whose moving truck caused a delay with his workers. Richard was struck by the look of her standing there, her dark hair soaking wet, her face with no makeup. Her dark eyes peered at him in despair.

She yelled against the noise of the storm; lightening flashing and thunder reverberating down the red rocks. "I tried to stop it, but...I...can't!"

He motioned to her, shouting. "Here, over here!"

He ran across the street and began shoveling rocks and mud out of a plugged culvert and she joined him, but her efforts were feeble compared to his strength. In a few moments, the water began moving back into the culvert and out of her driveway.

The rain subsided and soon stopped, leaving the two standing in a sea of red mud.

"What an awful mess!" she said as she wiped her face with her hand, leaving a muddy streak across her cheek.

Richard looked at her and smiled. He wondered how a woman with such despair in her eyes could look so beautiful.

"I wasn't referring to myself, although I bet I do look a mess," She laughed as she pushed wet hair back from her face.

"No, you don't. You look just fine." He was leaning on his shovel, still smiling at her, his deep green eyes visible behind his glasses.

Kathleen flashed a quick grin which he took as a sign of embarrassment. "I'm really grateful for your help. I don't know how to pay you for this, but..."

"Listen, that's my job. I was out with my men checking the sewer line. It's obvious our construction blocked the drainage channel. We were responsible for this, I'm sorry to say."

"Can I offer you a cup of coffee? You're as wet as I am." Her voice trembled a little.

"No thanks. I better get back to my men. I'm glad I was around to help you," he said.

"Yes, I'm glad you were, too." Kathleen reached out and shook his hand, feeling an unexpected jolt of warmth that made her long for more of his touch. Instead, she turned and walked back into her carport and sat down on the steps of the small porch to pull off her boots.

She watched as Richard headed toward his truck, but turned before he reached it, turned and came back to her. Kathleen noticed he looked as alone and cold as she was.

"I've got a couple hours of work left. Would you mind having dinner with me? Nothing special. I was just going to one of the coffee shops on the main boulevard. I really hate eating alone."

Kathleen looked into his direct gaze, and she felt a flutter in her chest.

"Yes, that would be fine," she answered. "I'll be waiting for you to pick me up."

They drove to the Coffee Pot Restaurant, a popular spot in West Sedona known for its 101 Omelets. The restaurant was filled with locals and tourists, and after a short wait, they were directed to a booth up against the wall. Even though it was late in the afternoon, Kathleen ordered a chorizo and cheese omelet and Richard decided on ham and eggs.

They exchanged the talk of strangers getting to know one another: The weather, the town, the influx of tourists. Suddenly, however, their conversation changed to more intimate subjects—he was tired of not being able to go home to Phoenix on the weekends. The job was not going well. Delays were constant, either with the breaking of utility and water lines or hitting hard rock which always took longer to dig out than anticipated.

She worried that moving back to Sedona from Phoenix was a bad decision. Her job was not what she had thought it would be. Maybe it would be better to go back to Los Angeles, near her mother.

Richard looked around the restaurant. It was plain the New Age community frequented it, many of them dressed as if they were in costume with odd looking hats, long flowing dresses, some carrying drums or flutes. "Seems like Sedona is not the place for either of us," he lamented.

Kathleen nodded her head in agreement and turned for a moment to watch an older woman—obviously Caucasian—saunter into the restaurant dressed as if she had just came off a western movie set. A band around her forehead held her dark hair from her face, she wore moccasins and scads of Navajo jewelry.

There was a note of exasperation in Richard's voice. "What's with some of these people in this town? They're sure a lot different than any I've seen in Phoenix. They dress funny.

What's their game?"

She laughed. "They're New Agers. I was just talking to someone I work with who is into their philosophy. She told me the New Age is a journey toward the love of God."

"I think they're just lost souls. They would be better off if they embraced Jesus Christ."

Kathleen, surprised by his comment, asked. "Are you a born-again Christian?"

"Yes, I'm born again." Richard said. "I received Jesus Christ into my life several years ago. I reached out to Him and He changed my life completely."

"And now you're saved?" she asked.

"Yes. I accepted Jesus as my savior and asked for the forgiveness of my sins. I've been accepted back into His loving arms."

Kathleen had a critical look on her face.

"You don't believe me?" Richard asked.

"Oh...I believe that you believe that. I just have a little trouble with the born-again Christian fundamentalist movement, the preachers who try to convert people to Jesus Christ while they're busy screwing old people out of their money. These people are so busy telling everyone else how to behave they've forgotten the Ten Commandments themselves, and that includes coveting thy neighbor's wife."

He laughed at her frank answer. "I agree with you that many of those so-called tele-evangelists are a discredit to the name of Jesus. But others work very hard and do a good job bringing the message of Christianity. I belong to a small church in Phoenix, and we just read the Bible and try to be good Christians."

"That's not easy in this day and age." Her voice had a note of hardness to it.

"You're not a Christian?"

"I guess you could say I'm a fallen-away Roman Catholic," she said, "but I always thought I was a Christian, too."

"Have you asked Jesus for forgiveness?"

"Well, of course, every time I've gone to confession."

"No. I don't mean that. What I mean is that you must be ready to give your life to Jesus by accepting Him as your personal savior. When we do that, we are born again because we are free from our past sins. We are cleansed. God can be counted upon to keep His word. He forgives us, no matter what we have done in the past."

"Well, if that's what you mean, then my answer is no. I'm a Christian but not born again."

Kathleen hadn't expected the conversation to turn to religion, a topic she was not in the mood to discuss, and the tone in her voice prompted Richard to say, "I didn't mean to offend you. You asked me if I was a born-again Christian and I told you. I know I don't seem like a good Christian when I ask you to dinner considering I'm married, but I admit to being only human and I needed to talk to someone. You seemed like you needed to talk too."

She softened. "I'm sorry if I seem edgy. These days, God seems very far away. All I want is some peace in my life. I haven't had that for a long time. I'm hoping that if I bury myself in my work, somehow, I'll make it through this tough period."

"I have no doubt you will. You seem like a strong woman. But you should pray. It will bring you closer to God and the peace you seek."

Although irritated with his preaching, inexplicably Kathleen was drawn to Richard. They remained silent as they finished their meal, and later when they arrived at her house, they walked into the backyard where they had a clear view of the Mogollon Rim above Oak Creek Canyon. The late summer monsoon storm had blown away and now the full moon was up over the canyon rim, showing the outline of the red rocks. Quietly, they stood in Kathleen's yard and looked at the moon shining over Sedona.

"It's really quite beautiful here, though isn't it?" she asked him, as if continuing their conversation from the restaurant. "Despite all our problems."

As she looked toward him, she saw a shooting star streak across the bright sky. "Look! Oh, I've never seen one so big before! Its tail stretches all across the sky!"

Richard laughed. "You're something! Do you know that?" He reached out and pulled her to him, kissing her hard, wrapping her into his body with his strong arms.

He had taken her by surprise. At first she didn't know how to respond. She let him kiss her, but his passion caught up with her and she returned his kiss that told of her yearning.

Finally he let her go. They stood for a moment, facing one another. Richard's voice was soft. "My God! I shouldn't have done that, but I couldn't help myself. You're so appealing to me. I've thought about you since the first time I saw you. When I saw you again today, standing out here in the rain, all I wanted to do was to help you."

"And now, what do you want, Richard?"

"I think you know."

"Yes, I do. I want it too. I'm lonely and feeling sorry for myself. But for you, it would be a disaster. You're married and you've changed your life by taking up the mantle of Christianity.

You better think twice about this." She kissed him lightly on the forehead. "Besides, it's the moonlight."

"And you. What about you?" He took her hand and kissed her softly on the palm. She could feel herself melt, but she held on, fighting the heat rising in her.

"I don't know about me. I haven't known about me for a long time."

CHAPTER 15

MEMO

To: Kathleen Sullivan
From: Jack Berens
Subject: The Sedona scene at one of the big resorts

How about an interview with someone who works at one of those pricey resorts? What's it like working where the high rollers come to spend their dough? Find someone with a tale to tell that is different from the public relations garbage thrown out by the chamber of commerce.

Maureen Randall
"Everything Just Perfect"
By Kathleen Sullivan
The *Sedona Chronicle*

ometimes, Maureen Randall feels like an airline stewardess in her trim blue uniform.

There's a problem with that analogy of her job, however. As Maureen sees it, her job as concierge at Las Brisas, one of Sedona's lush resorts, is similar to that of an airline stewardess only because she serves the public. Unfortunately, she isn't flying around the world visiting exotic places like Rome or Cairo like she would if she were working for an airline. Sedona isn't Rome or Cairo in Maureen's book.

Maureen leans on her elbow and speaks in a low voice so no one will hear her complaint. Only the water splashing in the lobby fountain can be heard.

"There are days when I think if I answer one more question about these red rocks, I'll spit. It wouldn't be so bad if the questions were not the same, but they are! They want to know where the best views are, where Red Rock Crossing is, where the Chapel of the Holy Cross is, where Airport Mesa is... on and on and on and on! Oh, and yes--they want to know which the best and cheapest Jeep tour is."

It's been a long four years for Maureen. She loved her job when she first got it, she says, because she loves talking to people from different walks of life. But the same questions are now driving her crazy. The questions and her standard of living are making her think she should go back home to Cincinnati where she formerly worked as concierge at the stately Cincinnatian Hotel.

"I love Cincinnati. It's a city you can sink your teeth into. I feel this horrible need to ride in an elevator to the top of a 30-story skyscraper, look out over the beautiful Ohio River and see a real forest! Not this juniper and pinon pine stuff they call a forest here in Sedona."

Maureen sighs. She's thinking of her hometown's annual Oktoberfest. "I just want to drink a beer and eat good German food, you know—sausage, and sauerkraut and potatoes—and dance the crazy chicken or a polka."

A divorcee with a 10-year-old daughter, Maureen has roomed with two older women since she moved to Sedona. Lots of people who come to Sedona end up renting a room because they can't afford the high cost of housing, she says.

"With my salary, renting a house in Sedona for myself and my daughter is out of the question. Oh, I guess I could live in Cottonwood or Cornville where housing is a lot cheaper, but I don't like my daughter being so far away from me. Geez, but there sure are times when I crave my own privacy. I get so tired of listening to my roommates' New Age music—you know those East Indian cymbals and Native American flutes that's all the rage in Sedona. I grew up with disco music, the Bee Gees, but I'm outvoted at the house. No one wants to listen to what I like to hear!"

Maureen's other gripe is the lack of men her own age.

"Oh, there's eligible men here all right! But they're old geezers looking for someone to take them to the doctor."

Her job isn't difficult, Maureen says, and sometimes it's even fun. She remembers getting a big tip when she arranged a picnic for an elderly judge who wanted to surprise his young wife. Maureen ordered the best French wine, caviar, cheeses, and crusty French bread, and coaxed the hotel chef to make chocolate eclairs for dessert. She even wrangled a blanket from the hotel laundry for the picnic.

"That guy was so smitten, that after the picnic he came in and gave me a $50 tip! Frankly, I think the young wife gave the judge a favor or two out there in the forest."

Maureen straightens up. A hotel guest is walking toward her. She fusses with her black tie and puts on a smile. Maureen wears her blond hair short and curly. It accents her cheery blue eyes and bright attitude.

"Good morning, I'm Maureen. Can I help you?"

The woman, who is in her 40s and wearing a large black T-shirt over black tights, has a scowl on her face.

"Yeah. Are you the concierge?" Her voice is sullen.

There is a sign on Maureen's desk that plainly identifies her, but she answers the woman politely. "Yes, I am."

"I made reservations by phone a couple weeks ago for one of those off-road Jeep tours, and now they tell me they're canceling the trip because of the heavy rains here during the past few days. I don't know what rain has to do with my Jeep trip." There's a note of disgust in the woman's voice as she pops her gum.

Maureen clears her throat, and attempts to explain the situation carefully. "The Jeep tours run in the National Forest, only on the approval of the Forest Service. After several days of heavy summer rain like we've had lately, the roads are assessed by the Forest Service and the Jeep companies, and if they believe damage will be done to the off-road trails, the tours are halted until the roads dry."

"Yeah, but this is my only day here. I don't care about the road! I want that Jeep ride I saw in the brochure, you know the scary one where the Jeep looks like it's going down steps." The woman fiddles with a multitude of thick gold chains around her neck.

Maureen answers politely, her hands clasped tightly together on top of her desk. "There are other Jeep trips where you can get a fine view of Sedona, only they go in areas where the terrain won't be damaged. I would be happy to make other arrangements for you."

The woman's upper lip curls in anger. "You don't understand. I want to take that trip that I made reservations for. Are you telling me the Jeep company won't do it?"

"I'm afraid so. If the tour company runs their Jeeps after heavy rains in an area that could be damaged, their permit to operate could be pulled by the Forest Service."

The woman takes a deep breath and repeats herself. "You don't understand! I have this new American Express Gold Card and I want to use it all I can while I'm here in Sedona! I should be able to take that Jeep ride. It's sunny out today, for God's sake! I wanted everything just perfect on this trip and I'm not getting it!"

Seeing that the woman does not want to listen to her explanation, Maureen tries to placate the guest. "May I have your name and suite number, please? I'll call the company and see if they have any trips scheduled this afternoon. Perhaps the sun has dried out the trails."

"Yeah? Well, OK. I'm Jamie Smythe. I'm in room 116," she says, digging the room key out of her large designer handbag. She drops the key on the desk.

Maureen dials the number of the Jeep tour company. "Hi, Annie, this is Maureen Randall. I have a guest here at the resort who is quite upset that the off-road tour she made reservations for several weeks ago has been canceled because of the rain."

"Is it that Smythe woman?" Annie asks.

"Yes."

"Lord, who do some of these people think they are anyway! I've been on the phone with her twice already. So she decided to give you a try, huh?"

Maureen looks up at Jamie and gives her a pleasant smile while cradling the phone close to her ear. "Yes, she did, Annie," she says in a sing-song tone, dying to say more, but knowing she couldn't dare. "I'm wondering—is there any possibility of you running that off-road tour this afternoon?"

"No. Our men went out this morning to look at the road, but it's much too wet. I explained that to her already."

"Do you have any suggestions, Annie, as to how we can help Ms. Smythe?"

"Well, aside from telling her to go take a leap off Bell Rock and a few other niceties, I can only give her a trip at sunset where the tour will take in the view from Airport Mesa and the Chapel of the Holy Cross. But it's not off-road. At this time of the day, everything else is all booked up. If she doesn't make up her mind soon, she's going to miss out on everything."

"Yes, I know. Hold on, Annie—Ms. Smythe, the only open trip scheduled is at sunset where you will be taken to Airport Mesa which will give you a lovely view of Sedona, and to the Chapel of the Holy Cross which looks toward Bell Rock and Courthouse Butte. It's a fun trip and you would get a good look at the red rocks, particularly at sunset."

The woman stamps her foot like a little girl. "I can't believe this! Who gives a damn about the ruts in the road? I sure don't. I'm ready to give them my new American Express Gold Card and they don't want it!"

Maureen stares at the women for a moment and then says into the phone, "Annie, hold on a minute will you?"

"Sure, Maureen. I'm listening carefully to this fascinating conversation."

Maureen looks up at the hotel guest in a businesslike manner and takes a deep breath.

"Ms. Smythe. The people who run those Jeep tours care about the roads because they have the Forest Service on their ass. The Forest Service cares about the roads because they have the public on their ass. And the people who live here care about the roads because of inconsiderate asses like you. If everyone who came here thought like you, Sedona would fast disappear into a cloud of red dust. Now, do you or do you not want a ride at sunset?"

Janie Smythe flushes red with anger, like the rocks she longs to see.

"I want to see the manager of this hotel. I don't like your attitude!"

Maureen returns to the telephone. "Thanks for your help, Annie."

"Sure, kid. Hope your day runs better than it is now."

"Ms. Smythe?" Maureen says hanging up the phone. "The hotel manager's name is Martin Layton. He'd be happy to talk to you. Just go over to the front desk and ask for him."

The woman grabs her hotel key and turns on her heel, her large gold earrings swinging with her abrupt movement.

Maureen readjusts her tie as she watches Ms. Smythe storm across the lobby.

She heaves a sigh. "You know what? I could be fired for that comment I just made, but I just couldn't help myself. I guess you could say this is one of those days when I really do wish I were an airline stewardess. That way, I could at least fantasize about opening up an exit and shoving the bitch out the plane, and you can quote me on that!"

CHAPTER 16

O n her way home from work, Kathleen stopped at the Safeway supermarket in West Sedona to buy groceries. The store was full of Sedona residents and people who were camping in the canyon. She could always tell the difference because the campers usually wore fanny packs and bought hot dogs, chips, beer, and charcoal briquettes.

While waiting in line, Kathleen's friend and former neighbor, Marlene Fisher, came up behind her and tapped her on the shoulder.

"Hi, Kathleen. Long time no see. Where have you been keeping yourself? All I know about you is from the articles I read in the *Chronicle* which, by the way, are terrific. Everyone in town is talking about them."

Kathleen gave her a hug. Marlene's slim figure was dressed in a gaudy tight floral print outfit. Her flaming red hair was pulled back in a matching bow, and she was covered with dangling, expensive jewelry.

"I'm sorry. I've been keeping pretty much to myself since I moved back. I'm still trying to finish unpacking, and it's taking me longer than expected. I guess I just don't have the heart to fix the place up, somehow."

"What's the matter, Kathleen? You sound really down."

Kathleen looked around, making sure there was no one within hearing distance.

"I've got a court hearing coming up soon in Phoenix. It's about Scott's will, and all the Buckleys will be there. God, how I hate to be anywhere near that bunch! There are a few other things, too. I should come over some day and cry on your shoulder. I think I need it...but it's hard to come back to your house since it's so close to where I lived with Scott."

"I know it is, Kathleen. I understand. Say, what day is the hearing?"

"October first."

"Why don't I ride down with you? You could use some company in court besides your lawyer."

Kathleen brightened. "Oh, Marlene! Would you? I really could bend your ear going and coming."

"Good. I'll talk to you before then."

"Thanks, Marlene. I appreciate your thoughtfulness."

Kathleen let out a sigh of relief. Maybe the day in Phoenix won't be so terrible after all, she thought.

After spending more than $80 on groceries, most of it on staples she had not bought since she moved back to town, Kathleen wearily pushed the cart out to the parking lot and unloaded the bags into the trunk of her car.

Shoving the cart over to the storage area, she passed a new convertible with the top town. Kathleen noticed the license plate was from New York, and something strange was sticking up in the back seat. She stopped to look at it, but she couldn't figure out what the object was.

"Hi," someone said.

Surprised, Kathleen turned around. Standing behind her was a couple, both in their fifties. They had on T-shirts that read, "Pyramid Power is the Way and the Light."

The man wore his gray hair in a ponytail. "Were you looking at our pyramid?"

"Oh, is that what it is? I just saw it sticking out from your back seat," Kathleen said.

"Would you like to see it?"

Never wanting to miss an opportunity to learn something new, Kathleen nodded.

The man, who introduced himself as Horace, picked it up from the back seat and put it on top of the car trunk. On his right hand, Kathleen noticed a large gold ring in the shape of a pyramid. The object he placed on the car was an open-sided pyramid, made of gold-colored rods. Hanging in the middle of the pyramid was a large crystal.

"What do you use it for?" Kathleen reached out to touch the beautiful crystal, but Horace stopped her.

"I don't mean to be rude, but if you touch the crystal, you'll change the energy. It's my crystal and has my energy."

"Oh, I'm sorry! I didn't know." Kathleen said. I'm fascinated by this. Tell me how you use it."

"We believe Pyramid Power is the medium to be used to reach our highest level of energy, to the Way and the Light. We meditate under it. See? It fits on my head."

After he took it off, he continued. "The pyramid channels energy from the universe to us as we meditate to reach our higher selves." Horace's companion nodded, smiling.

"Why do you have a crystal in the middle?"

"That's to increase the energy even more. We each have our own crystal." Horace lightly touched his companion.

Sensing a scam, Kathleen said, "Gee, I guess I must be living in the dark ages. I've heard about pyramid power, but never paid much attention. How do you know about all this pyramid, energy stuff?"

"We've been at a seminar here for the past week," the woman answered. Her straight black hair was pulled away from her face, which Kathleen could see was scarred from acne.

"A seminar? On pyramid power?"

The woman continued. "Oh, yes. See our T-shirts? The person holding the seminar is world-renowned—Dr. Wallace Ostrov. We've been waiting for months to attend. We've driven from New York and plan to stay another week in Sedona just to practice using the pyramid properly. You know, climb around on the vortex sites and meditate. Then we can go home and continue to become more attuned to our higher selves. Through this, we will gain fame, fortune and eternal life."

"Really? My, this is interesting." Kathleen said. "I'm curious. Would you mind telling me how many people attended the seminar?"

"About 50. People from all over the world. I understand Dr. Ostrov holds one every week," Horace answered. "Not just in Sedona, but all over the world."

"I would be interested in attending something like that. Is it expensive?" Kathleen hoped to pull more information from the couple.

Horace nodded. "Well, I suppose you could say $3,000 apiece is expensive, but we know we're going to use this and be all the better for it." The woman smiled, acknowledging the knowledge she had gained.

"Well, thank you for telling me about this." Kathleen made a movement toward her car, hoping to break off the conversation from the two pyramid pilgrims. She was tired and wanted to go home.

"You're welcome. We hope you plan to attend Dr. Ostrov's seminar. Your life will be changed forever," the woman said, still smiling.

Kathleen nodded in response and climbed into her car. Yeah, I'll just bet, she thought.

As Kathleen turned down her street and glanced in her rearview mirror. Richard's truck turned the corner behind her and followed her into her driveway.

She got out of her car, opened the trunk, and began pulling out the plastic bags filled with groceries. Richard walked toward her and she looked at him, feeling her loneliness flood over her.

My, God, she thought, I'm so glad to see him!

"Let me help," he said, grabbing three bags in each hand. The feeling of having someone help her was one she had forgotten. She felt a flicker of gratitude.

They walked in through her back porch and he put the groceries on her kitchen counter. Without a word, he began taking the groceries out of the bags, putting then in piles for the cupboard, refrigerator, freezer.

Kathleen stood in the middle of the kitchen floor, watching him in amazement. It was as if he suddenly belonged here in her home, and she didn't even know him. What was it about this man that filled her with such peace and fulfilment?

Suddenly, he turned and faced her. He put his arms around her and kissed her. It was a long, lingering kiss.

His voice was husky. "I thought about what you said the other night. I've done nothing but think about it, about you, and my answer is that I'm here."

Kathleen closed her eyes for a moment, afraid of what she just heard, afraid his appearance was just a dream. When she opened her eyes, he was still there, his eyes searching her face for an answer. Her will power to stop what she knew was going to happen evaporated. She needed an end to this terrible loneliness, if only for a moment. She was overwhelmed with that thought, and she gave in to her desire, taking his hand and leading him to her bedroom.

It was as if they had been lovers for many years. Neither was embarrassed as they undressed in the twilight, the last rays of the sun coming in through her window. Richard looked at her as she stood before him naked. He smiled that smile that always warmed her.

"My God, you are beautiful," he said as he pulled her to him and entered into her. She gave a short cry of delight.

"It's been so long for me," she whispered, moving to the rhythm of his body.

He kissed her in the cove of her neck, sending an electrical charge throughout her.

"Well, then. All the more reason why it should be so pleasurable."

Kathleen melted into him, feeling his body inside hers. Suddenly, waves of pleasure flooded over her and she arched her back wanting it to last longer. He realized she wanted more and began moving faster and deeper into her. Kathleen moaned softly as she reacted to his movements. When he knew she was done, his passion surfaced and blossomed.

Afterward, he rained kisses on her face. "You've captured me."

She ran her finger along his facial features, tracing them into the crevice of her mind. "Well, for the time being anyway," she said softly."

She sighed, trying to avoid her thoughts now that the passion had died and her conscience was turned back on. Somehow, Kathleen knew instinctively the consequences of this passionate involvement.

CHAPTER 17

MEMO

To: Kathleen Sullivan
From: Jack Berens
Subject: The homeless

There's a hell of a lot of lost souls who roam around Sedona by day and sleep in the forest at night. I know you've seen the same ones I have—those who walk endlessly up and down the city sidewalks, others who live in makeshift campers on top of their ragged trucks or in their cars crammed with every belonging.

These forest people must have some other reason why they come here, aside from the mild weather and beauty. What do they do all day—meditate at a prayer circle or hunt through trash bins? Find out.

Elizabeth Stark
"Never Seen a Place So Beautiful"
By Kathleen Sullivan
The *Sedona Chronicle*

E lizabeth Stark spends most of her days walking though Sedona.

Elizabeth is one of those nameless, faceless people the media calls homeless. But she doesn't feel homeless, despite what people think about her ragged appearance. That's because Elizabeth has made her home in the National Forest on the outskirts of Sedona.

She doesn't own any form of transportation, so she walks along the main highways of Sedona, keeping to herself, looking for food behind supermarkets, going through trash bins early in the morning before the garbage trucks rumble through town. On Wednesdays, she's the first one in line at the Sedona Food Bank.

Elizabeth is dirty. Her face has red dirt smudged on it, and her coal-black hair is stringy, although she keeps it as tidy as she can by pulling it back into a ponytail. It's apparent she doesn't own a comb because her hair is tangled.

"At least, it's out of my face. I know it don't look all that good, but it's out of my face," she says, touching her hair, her voice showing defiance.

Elizabeth's clothes are old and spotted, although she washes them in Oak Creek, using the time-worn method of beating them with a rock. Sometimes, she gets used clothing at the Food Bank, but she tries to keep only enough clothing to carry on her back in case she's forced to move quickly from her camp.

There's also a smell about Elizabeth. It's a mixture of dirt, campfire smoke, and some peculiar oil she wears on her skin in an effort to hide the smell that trails after her.

"I try to wash myself up in Oak Creek, too, but that water is cold," she says, shaking her head realizing no one ever stands close to her, even at the food bank.

Elizabeth looks down at her hands which are rough because she has no hand lotion. Her fingernails are broken and dirty. It's been a long time since she's been in a beauty salon, if she ever has.

At 33 years old, Elizabeth admits she is down and out, but there are some compensations for living in the forest. "I've a nice little camp that protects me from the wind and rain, and I've hidden it well enough this time so those damn forest cops haven't found it! I have a simple life. No bills, and no bill collectors like I had after me when I lived in California. I get food from the trash bins and the Sedona Food Bank, ya know? What more is there?"

She had a good job once, she says, working on an assembly line for a Southern California packaging company that closed about a year ago. The company moved to a Third World nation, a country whose name Elizabeth can't pronounce.

"I couldn't get another job 'cause that's all I know how to do. I'm one of those high school dropouts, ya know, and I don't want to go to none of those government programs where they teach ya how to become a computer what-ever-it-is. That's just not for me."

Elizabeth scratches her head and continues her story. "After I lost my job, my car was taken away, and I got kicked out of my furnished apartment. I just left most of my stuff behind and packed one bag. The only way out of Hawthorne was to hitchhike. I thought if I got to another area of the country, I could find me a job, but I had no luck in Phoenix either."

Elizabeth doesn't talk about the few months she spent in Phoenix. "Those are mean streets in that town. Man, I had some trouble there, so I hitched a ride with a truck driver about six months ago who was goin' north and he dropped me off at a McDonald's in a place called Camp Verde. I walked 'til I got into Cottonwood and then some old man gave me a lift into Sedona. God! I never seen a place so beautiful in my life, although I never been anywheres but California. The red cliffs here are spiritual, ya know? Don't laugh, I really believe that. I found me some peace here." She taps her heart.

Her large hat, which resembles the kind worn by Chinese coolies who built the railroads of the American West, flops about her head when the wind blows as she walks Sedona's sidewalks.

"I get tired of walkin', but there ain't nothin' else to do. I can't lay by the creek all day or read 'cause I can't read very well neither, so I just'd rather be walkin'."

And so Elizabeth can be seen hoofing it through town most any day of the week. Sometimes she considers using her thumb to hitch a ride, but she's afraid the Sedona Police will pick her up for being a vagrant.

She won't say where she lives because she knows the enforcement officers of the Coconino National Forest are always looking for her small camp. That's why she leaves early in the morning and goes back to it after dark. If they find her camp with her there, she knows they will arrest her and haul her off to jail in Flagstaff.

That's happened to her once already, but she managed to bum a ride back down the canyon with some Navajos who were coming into Sedona to sell jewelry to store owners in Uptown.

"Those guys with the Forest Service, they can be real mean if they want to, ya know? They're really nothin' but cops, ya know, forest cops. They wear guns, too, imagine that in a forest. I know they'd love to get rid of me, but this is where I live, and this is where I'll stay 'til the weather forces me out."

Elizabeth arrived in Sedona in late spring. Now that the nights are beginning to get chilly, she's not sure if she can survive a hard winter in Sedona, like everyone seems to be predicting.

She shrugs her shoulders, again showing a flash of defiance. "Ya never know, it might be a mild winter."

"I've never lived where there's snow, being from California and all. If it gets too cold, I may have to hitch south, somewhere where it's warm, like near the border, ya know? Maybe that place called Yuma would be the place to go."

But although it may be warmer and easier for her to survive the winter near the border, Elizabeth says she will always return to Sedona.

"My heart's here. I ain't gonna live no where else, forest cops or no forest cops. This is my home."

CHAPTER 18

Kathleen poured her heart out to Marlene on their way to the probate hearing in Phoenix, but the more she talked, the more nervous she became. She bore down on the freeway as if she were late for her own funeral.

Marlene tenderly touched her friend. "Kathleen, relax! Look at you! Your shoulders are tight as a drum."

As she pulled off the freeway and headed toward Maricopa County Superior Court, Kathleen acknowledged Marlene's concern. "I know! I know! The hearing is bad enough, but seeing those damn Buckleys is something I never wanted again in my life. Oh, Lord! Why do I even have to be there?"

The closer she drove to the courthouse, the more her stomach began to bother her, but she said nothing to Marlene, hopeful that the feeling would simply go away. After several trips around the block, Kathleen finally found a spot to park her car.

"I have a feeling about this hearing, Marlene. It's not a good feeling."

"I hope you're wrong, Kathleen."

Marlene stepped out of Kathleen's car as if she just stepped out of a salon. Her red hair, red nails and makeup with matching lipstick were done to perfection. She wore an expensive gray suit with a white silk blouse. A large mabe pearl pin was clasped to the lapel of the suit, and her earrings matched the exquisite pin.

Kathleen glanced at her friend. She remembered looking as stylish as Marlene, but those days of lavish spa treatments and facials were no longer available to her. She felt a pang, a longing for what her life had once been. Somehow, looking fashionable was not a mandatory requirement in her life these days. She felt lucky just to get up and out of bed, dogged by the depression that haunted her.

Kathleen wore a pink suit with a blouse the same shade, both bought at a large discount store in Flagstaff. Kathleen's dark hair was pulled back in a bun at the nape of her neck, her makeup was slight, only pink lipstick and mascara, and her nails were unpolished. The only jewelry she wore were small pearl earrings.

Dan Harris, Kathleen's attorney, was waiting by the bank of elevators inside the court building. A short, heavy set middle-aged man with thinning hair, Dan was thumping his fingers nervously against his briefcase.

After introducing Marlene, Kathleen asked, "Is the hearing to contest the will?"

"I'm afraid so. I got notification of that yesterday just before my office closed. I knew something was up after talking to Price that day, but the court documents filed initially for this hearing only stated it was a meeting for the beneficiaries to discuss the estate's assets with the judge.

He sighed heavily. "I've been in a whirlwind this morning, preparing papers asking the court to postpone this hearing. This is very irregular, Kathleen."

She nodded, innately understanding more than Dan even knew. A cold feeling moved down her spine, and she took several short breaths.

Seeing her look, Dan placed his hand on her shoulder. "Are you OK?"

"Dan...Could I sit down for just a moment?" She took another deep breath as she sat on a bench near the elevators. Her face looked drawn.

He glanced at his watch. "For just a moment, Kathleen. The hearing is set for 10 a.m. Judge Oswald is a stickler for punctuality."

He moved closer to her. "I know what this means to you financially, Kathleen. I will try my best, but I don't think we have a chance if they wish to pursue Scott's alcoholism. He may have died because he hit the ice pocket at high speed and crashed into the bridge, but the autopsy showed his blood alcohol level to be twice above the legal limit. I want you to be prepared for the worst."

She nodded, stood up and took another deep breath.

"Let's get this over with, then."

They rode up to the third floor and entered Judge Oswald's quiet, thickly carpeted courtroom, which gave off an odor of newness. Philip Buckley turned as they entered, giving Kathleen a scowl. Beside him was his attorney, Ross Price, who had not aged a day since he coaxed her those many years ago into signing the prenuptial agreement before she married Scott. On the other side of Price was Jessica and Natalie Buckley. They did not look at her.

Kathleen, Marlene and Dan sat on the opposite side of the aisle with Kathleen placing herself the farthest from the Buckleys.

A few minutes later, Kathleen felt a tap on her shoulder. She looked around to find Jason Cox, a young reporter she knew from the *Arizona Republic*.

"Well, hi, Jason. What brings you here?"

The young man grinned. "You're kidding, Kathleen."

She tried to understand his meaning. "Is there some big case coming up on the docket after this hearing?"

"Come on Kathleen! You know a news story when you see one! The Buckleys are prominent people in this state considering they own one of the largest Arizona-based corporations. It's hot news that they want to reveal their brother was an alcoholic just to get you off the will!"

She sat looking at him for a moment, stunned by his statement. "Yes," she said quietly. "I guess I never thought about it in that light—as a reporter, I mean. I'm too close to it. You're right, Jason, it is hot news."

She turned and faced the courtroom, trying to physically separate herself from the reporter. Her stomach again felt queasy. She dropped her head a little, focusing on the carpet pattern as a way to get through her feeling of utter hopelessness against the forces of Buckley power and prestige.

The judge entered the courtroom from a door in the back of the room and sat down at the bench, adjusting his robe.

"Mr. Price and Mr. Harris, will you please step up to the bench?" he asked both attorneys. They got up from their seats and then stood in front of the judge.

"I have read the argument and supporting evidence regarding Scott Buckley's alcoholism. It's a rather amazing collection of facts—in and out of alcoholic rehabilitation programs during the last two years of his life, and to no avail. I also understand that members of the Buckley family are willing to testify to those facts," he said, looking at Price.

The attorney nodded.

Kathleen's head jerked up. "That's a lie! The bastard never attended a rehabilitation program in his life!" she said loud enough for everyone in the courtroom to hear.

Jessica and Natalie Buckley turned and glared at her. Philip gave Kathleen a vicious smile.

Judge Oswald stopped and looked across the room at her. She pursed her lips to silence herself, knowing another outburst would only anger the judge, and Marlene put her hand on Kathleen's shoulder to comfort her. She put her head down, again staring at the carpet.

"I find it peculiar that after so many years of marriage to Kathleen Sullivan, the late Mr. Buckley finally decided to change his will, adding Mrs. Buckley during a time of his life when his alcoholism had a strong hold on him. I'm not inferring, mind you, that Mrs. Buckley had influenced him to change his will. Nevertheless, it does seem to me that he was not of sound mind when he did it."

"Your Honor!" interjected Dan. "These papers regarding the contest of the will were not presented to me until yesterday, as you can see by my brief. I respectfully request a postponement of this hearing in order to have time to adequately represent my client."

The judge took off his glasses. "Yes, I realize that, Mr. Harris. Unfortunately, it has taken almost six months to move this case into the heavy probate load of this court, and I understand that there is a land negotiation between the estate's executor, Philip Buckley, and the U.S. Forest Service over property Scott Buckley owned. A postponement could only cause problems with that delicate negotiation."

"But your Honor! This is highly irregular..." Harris nearly shouted.

The judge raised his hand in a motion that caused Harris to bite his lip. "Mr. Harris, I said I realize your concerns. I really do. But I understand these negotiations are quite critical with the U.S. Government and we need to resolve this as soon as possible. Therefore, my judgment is that the will of Scott Buckley be declared null and void. I declare the beneficiaries of the estate to be Scott Buckley's two daughters, Jessica and Natalie Buckley, and Scott Buckley's brother, Philip, who will also act as executor of the estate."

Judge Oswald banged his gavel, and Dan Harris' anger showed as he jammed one fist into his open hand. Kathleen did not look up. She sat still, her gaze never leaving the pattern of the rug under her feet, which seemed to be moving in waves along with the sick feeling in her stomach.

Dan Harris strode back to her, his eyes blazing. "This is fixed! As an attorney, I've never seen anything so dirty in my life!"

As he spoke, she lurched forward and his strong arm caught her by the shoulder. She tried to stop herself from vomiting, but she could not. Kathleen choked the contents of her stomach onto the plush carpet.

Marlene grabbed tissues from her purse and began wiping Kathleen's mouth.

"Oh, God. I'm so sorry. I'm so sorry," Kathleen kept saying, trying to clean herself. She never noticed the exit of the Buckleys who looked at her in disdain or that Jason Cox was scrambling after Philip to get a quote about the judge's ruling.

As Dan and Marlene helped her out to the hall, the bailiff, a fat man who savored his importance in the courtroom, stood cursing her. He picked up the telephone receiver on his desk and angrily punched in a number as he unconsciously fingered the revolver at his side.

"Hey, Mike! Send the janitor to Judge Oswald's courtroom. Now! Some bimbo just threw up on the new carpet."

CHAPTER 19

MEMO

To: Kathleen Sullivan
From: Jack Berens
Subject: Tourists

More than 4 million tourists a year flock to Sedona. Considering the massive marketing of this place by the chamber, the resorts, and the New Age community, the tourist industry can only get bigger, much to the delight of city officials who depend on tourist dollars for city improvements.

Grab one of those tourists and find out what's so great about this place.

Angie Dorian and her two sons, Chris and Steve
"It Doesn't Get Better Than This"
By Kathleen Sullivan
The *Sedona Chronicle*

A ngie Dorian parks her car on the side of the canyon highway, above Side Rock State Park, and begins walking with her two sons, 11-year-old Chris, and 9-year-old Steve, along a narrow trail with dozens of other tourists.

Everyone is heading to the park site where kids and gown-ups alike slide down slippery rocks amid the cold rushing water of Oak Creek.

The clear, bright day is a delight for Angie and the boys, who live in the smog-filled San Gabriel Valley near Los Angeles.

Angie, who is a single mother, says she needed to get away for a week from the bank where she works. She planned the trip over the Columbus Day holiday so Chris and Steve would only lose four days from school.

Angie carefully picks her way down the narrow path that leads to Oak Creek. She doesn't care much for heights, and the path is steeper than she likes. A couple of times she grabs onto the shoulders of her oldest son, who is in front of her, trying to keep her balance. Steve, meanwhile, has scampered far ahead of them both.

"I've never visited northern Arizona, so this is a treat for us," Angie says. While admitting that she is not too thrilled with the steep trail, she's happy the boys are excited about the adventure.

Like every working mother, she worries about the amount of time she spends with her boys. She hopes this trip will make up for some of the hours she's had to work overtime lately.

Angie parked along Hwy. 89A because the parking lot for Slide Rock filled by mid-morning. The autumn holiday weekend has brought hundreds of visitors to Sedona and Oak Creek Canyon.

"I went to the Southern California Automobile Club and the nicest lady gave me all the directions I needed to get here. But I didn't know it would be so beautiful! Look at the change in the color of the trees! We don't have this in Southern California!"

The sumacs are turning red now in the canyon and the cottonwoods are yellowing. Higher up the canyon, there are a few birch trees turning gold, their leaves like droplets of shimmering coins fluttering in the autumn breeze.

The trail begins to level off and Angie tells Chris to run ahead and find his brother.

"Hey, Mom, this is neat!" Chris yells as he runs down the trail and catches a view of the creek.

Visitors lie stretched out on the red rocks, soaking up the hot Indian Summer sun. Kids are laughing and splashing one another as they slip and slide down the rocks made smooth by the rushing water.

Chris drops his towel on a rock and takes off his socks, putting his tennis shoes back on.

"I think that's a good idea, Chris. The rocks might be sharp under the water," his mother says, spreading out her towel. Steve does the same as his brother, hurrying to get into the water first.

She takes sun block out of a bag and begins slathering it on her arms, face and chest, already beginning to turn red from the hot sun.

"I haven't seen this much sun in a long time. There's always a haze in the San Gabriel Valley unless the Santa Ana winds are blowing. Oh, but it's so clear here! And just look at those beautiful red rocks. It doesn't get better than this," she says.

Angie watches her boys play in the water with the other children.

"Gee, you know they have one of those big water slide parks in San Dimas, near the freeway. But this is the real thing. Be careful, Chris!" she yells to her son who is rough housing with another boy about his age.

"Yeah," the other boy tells Chris. "We were here yesterday and a man cracked his head while he was playing with some other people and they had to send for the paramedics. He got hurt real bad."

"Do you come here often?" Chris asks his new-found friend.

"We live in Phoenix. It takes us a couple of hours to get up here. We come a lot, especially during the summer. It gets real hot in Phoenix then. Is this your first time in here"

"Yeah," Chris says. "My mom has always wanted to visit Arizona. I guess she read a lot of those western books when she was a kid—Zane somebody, I think. I can't remember. It's nicer here than I thought it would be. I wanted to go to the beach for our trip, but it's different here. We're staying at some cabins up the canyon. There's lots of squirrels and birds by the cabins. I like chasing the squirrels."

Steve, meanwhile has found an area away from the cold water where he can build a little dam with rocks. He's brought along some action figures and is having a game of war in the water.

After several hours of play, Chris scrambles back up the rocks to where Angie is sunning herself.

"Hungry?" she asks.

"Uh huh. The kids say there's a fast food place in town. Want to go there?"

"OK, let's go. There's another place I want to see while we're in Sedona. It's called Red Rock Crossing," Angie tells her son. She calls down to Steve, who reluctantly leaves his newly-built fortress.

"Can we come back, Mom?" Chris asks. "I really like it here."

"I think so. We've got time enough to do that tomorrow," she tells her son, mussing his hair, which is the same warm auburn as hers.

Angie enjoys feeling the warm fall breeze rustle her hair through the open window as she drives slowly down the canyon. Once in a while she catches a glimpse of the stark red canyon walls against the backdrop of the changing cottonwoods growing in the creek. At one point, they see a trout farm on the left hand side of the road, across the creek.

"Mom, Mom, look at that!" Chris shouts. "Hey, can we go fishing there?"

Angie slows down and stares for a moment at the road to the trout farm and the adjoining trailer park. She pulls over to the side of the roadway, carefully checking behind her for traffic.

"I don't know, guys," Angie says, eyeing the steep road that takes a deep dip to the left and crosses the creek at water level. "I don't much like that road down there. It looks dangerous to me, crossing that creek. Gosh! What must it be like in a flood?" she asks the question more to herself than to the boys.

"Maybe the turn won't be so bad coming up the canyon," she says finally, noting the name of the place—Rainbow Trailer Park and Trout Farm. As she drives toward Sedona she says half aloud, "Why in the name of God would anyone live there knowing they would have to cross that creek every day?"

An hour later, Angie pulls into the parking lot at Red Rock Crossing. Although they are miles downstream from Oak Creek Canyon, Red Rock Crossing is but another scenic spot along Oak Creek. They get out and walk to the picnic tables near the creek with their sack of hamburgers, fries and malts.

"Oh, my God! Isn't this beautiful?" Angie says, laying the sack on the table and walking closer to the creek. From there she gets a full view of Cathedral Rock, the same view seen on thousands of Arizona calendars, and in many of Hollywood's legendary westerns.

She pulls out her camera and takes a shot of the famous rock formation. In another photo, Angie catches her sons wading in the creek, eating their food. Chris has a silly grin on his face, and Steve is busy jamming French fries into his mouth, giggling.

It's a moment a mother remembers forever. Her boys are happy, and so is she.

"Like I said," Angie laughs, "it doesn't get better than this."

Chapter 20

It was 6:30 a.m. and the rays of the sun were just beginning to touch the tip of Capital Butte, one of Sedona's spectacular rock formations.

Just out of the shower, Kathleen put on her old green robe and wrapped her wet hair in a towel when she heard knocking on her back door.

She opened it to find Richard standing on her porch, wet with perspiration from his morning workout.

He smiled at her but his voice was serious. "Hi. I came over for a morning kiss."

Overwhelmed to see him after such a long absence, she was rendered speechless by his appearance. He walked into her service porch, put his keys on the washing machine and took her in his arms, kissing her all over her face, her lips, and her neck. He moved his hand inside her robe and felt her breast.

"My God, how beautiful you are in the morning!"

"Silly," she said, playfully pushing him away. "Want a cup of coffee?"

"No. I want you. I can't stay away from you, as hard as I try."

She laughed and led him to her bedroom where they tasted the delights of each other. Later, when they lay together, contented, she asked him why she had heard him swear when they were making love.

He laughed. "I knew you would ask. It must be the inquisitive reporter in you."

She pressed. "Well, why did you say 'damn you?'"

Richard turned serious. "It's because you're so delicious."

He paused and kissed her deeply. "You know, a woman can steal a man's soul."

"You're serious, aren't you?"

She was offended by his silence and pulled away from him. Kathleen got up from her bed and covered her nakedness with her robe.

"I'm not here to steal your soul, Richard. What has happened between us most certainly isn't right because you're married. But it has happened and it's not just a carnal attraction, at least not for me. Maybe it would be better for both of us if we stopped this right now, particularly if you think I have the ability to steal your soul. That sounds to me like some born-again Christian nonsense."

She turned and looked at him and then reached over, touching his bare chest, suddenly feeling dreadful because she had attacked his beliefs.

"It would be much better if we didn't see one another again because I'm falling in love with you. I'm at a terrible place in my life, Richard, and I'm vulnerable as hell. Falling in love with a married man will only cause me more grief on top of the grief I already carry in me." She spoke softly.

He reached out and pulled her to him.

"I've never done anything like this, Kathleen." Richard said softly. "I've been a faithful husband to my wife all these 30 years, even when I was away in the military. I know I wasn't the best husband because I drank a lot and hung around with the boys, but I never played around with other women."

His eyes filled with pain. "I can't explain what it is that I feel with you. It's like I've dreamed of you all my life. You're so beautiful, intelligent, and open to me. I've told you more about how I feel in the few times we have been together than I've told my wife in 30 years. I don't understand that. But we have—what's the term those shrinks use?"

"Bonded?"

"Yes, that's the word. It's like I've always known you, always loved you."

She kissed him lightly, thinking that those who believe in reincarnation would have a field day with Richard's admission.

"What are you saying?"

"That I want to be your lover."

"And what happens if it goes deeper than that? What happens if we fall so much in love with one another that we can't give each other up?"

"I don't know Kathleen, I just don't know. I haven't thought that far ahead. All I know is that I want you, not just physically, but that's a big part of it. I'm not denying that. But I also want to know you, your hopes and dreams. I want to take some of the pain away from your life, although I know I'm only adding to it." He stroked her hair.

"That's a big admission for a man who was headed for heaven one day, did a 180 degree turn and is now headed for hell because of your fall from grace."

He winced. "That's truer than you know. Don't you believe that we'll burn in hell because of what we're doing? I do." His voice was low, serious.

She didn't answer him for a moment. "Yet, you're willing to take the chance of that."

Richard put his eyes down, avoiding her gaze, her question. Suddenly, she felt overwhelmed at his acknowledgment of his obsession for her.

"In answer to your question," Kathleen said, "my response is no, I don't believe we'll burn in hell. I believe there's enough hell on this earth to go around without having to believe there's a hell after we die. As for heaven, it's only a dream man has conjured up to get through the scary night, the pain of life. If we think there's something better, then it makes the hardships of life a little easier to bear."

"I thought you said you were a practicing Catholic."

"Well, I was, Richard. I am no longer."

"What happened?"

"Reality forced me to look at the church differently than I had before."

"And because of that you look at God differently?"

"God? Oh, Richard! I do believe there is a God, a Creator. What I don't believe is this push that if you don't believe in Jesus Christ, no matter how good a person you are, you'll burn in hell. What about all those people who are fine and loving, trying every day to live truthful, honest lives— Buddhists, Muslims, Jews or those who just believe in the sacredness of the earth?"

Richard sat up from his lounging position. "No one is saved unless they believe in Jesus."

"See? You're like a recording," she answered.

"I pray someday you'll come to understand and believe what I believe." There was no anger in his voice, just hope.

But Kathleen became angry because of his placating tone and what she felt was the stupidity of his statement. She couldn't help herself from attacking his beliefs.

"I also don't believe this Christian nonsense that God answers every prayer. I think its crap when I hear a famous person, some football player saying in the locker room that God answered his prayer to win the Super Bowl. That's heresy! Why would anyone ask God for such a thing as unimportant as winning the Super Bowl or a PGA golf tournament?

He laughed. "Well, it's not that unimportant for thousands of people, I guess. What would you ask for?"

"For something important. World peace, to end the war in Bosnia, to stop the proliferation of drugs." She waved her hand to emphasize her words.

"But what would you ask for yourself, Kathleen?" he asked, curious.

She was silent for a moment.

"Maybe God already answered me," she said softly, stroking his forehead, sorry for her momentary anger. "I have you."

CHAPTER 21

MEMO

To: Kathleen Sullivan
From: Jack Berens
Subject: The Forest Service

I hear some bureaucrat from the U.S. Forest Service is retiring after almost 40 years as a ranger.

See if you can get this guy to open up about what his life has been like. I'm not interested in the usual promotional junk the Forest Service dishes out about how wonderful it is to save Smokey Bear.

Joel Miller
"Sometimes I Think I've Seen It All"
By Kathleen Sullivan
The *Sedona Chronicle*

J oel Miller wishes he had a dollar for every piece of trash he's picked up in the forest.

"Hell, I'd even take a dime for every piece of trash. I'd still be a multi-millionaire," Joel laments, taking off his Smokey Bear hat and scratching his bald head, looking over the red rocks from the top of Schnebly Hill Road.

Today, Joel is taking his weekly run up Schnebly Hill, looking for lost tourists, trash, troublemakers, and New Agers who insist on building prayer circles in the Coconino National Forest. That's Joel Miller's job as an enforcement officer for the U.S. Forest Service, Sedona Ranger District. In addition to his regular green uniform and his wide-brimmed hat, Joel also packs a firearm.

Joel is a man who loves to tell stories, particularly stories about this forest that he's protected for so many years.

The ranger places his foot on a rock to give him some balance and hitches up his gun belt. As if to give some perspective on his views, he looks toward the community of Sedona from the top of the hill, continues to scratch his bald head, and begins his story.

"It's getting near the end of the season, now. There aren't so many visitors because the nights are getting too chilly to camp out. This time of the year, though, people drive this road just to see the change in the fall colors. They seem to forget that you can run into real trouble on this rough rocky dirt road."

He squints against the low autumn sun and then chuckles. "Last week, I came across this couple from Germany who spoke very little English. They'd rented one of those slinky foreign cars and were sitting here in the middle of Schnebly Hill Road, stopped dead. They'd been driving too fast—probably thought they were on the Autobahn—and they'd gone over one of those big rock bumps in the road and ripped up the oil pan."

He shakes his head. "And all the way from Germany, too."

Joel, a man in his late 50's, has lived all of his life in or near Sedona, and is the scion of one of Sedona's oldest families. A big man, tall with broad shoulders, he carries himself proud, kind of a John Wayne type. He's not to be messed with, considering his bulk and his imposing stature. That's how he got into the enforcement end of the U.S. Forest Service—his size—he says. He also got into the Forest Service because it was the only place to get a decent job nearly 40 years ago.

"I'm no puny guy, I guess you can see. That's why I'm here, gun and all. I look kind of imposing to those people who come out here to make trouble, those who come to take away the beauty of the red rocks."

Joel Miller says he's seen all kinds of human behavior. "Yeah, sometimes, I think I've seen it all, right here in Sedona. There's been accidents—like the time a few years ago when a car full of teenagers went off the side of the cliff, right about here. Oh, that was a terrible thing to see! There's been plane crashes. One plane we didn't find for nearly eight months, and we found that only because a logger came across some bear dung with pieces of material in it that matched the hat of the guy flying the airplane!"

Joel shifts a little and continues his tale. "We've hunted escaped convicts like Danny Ray Horning though this forest, rounded up homeless people living illegally here, and done our best to prevent crime. But it's here, just like everywhere in America. People come to the red rocks to have a good time, and sometimes they get bothered by scum just like anywhere else."

Joel's view of New Agers is one of endurance. "God, but they do dress up in their weird costumes, trying to look like Indians—I mean Native Americans," he says, smiling about his politically incorrect slip. "It must irritate real Native Americans to see these strange folks running around the forest beating tom toms and playing their flutes."

Joel reaches in his top left-hand shirt pocket and pulls out a pack of small cigars. He chews off the end and jams it into his mouth without lighting it, obviously thinking about his next words.

"These New Agers come out here and build their rock circles and we dismantle them as soon as we can find them. We don't like them because they change the natural landscape. But they keep building them and we keep tearing them down. It's like a game we play with each other."

He admits to having strong opinions about the desecration of ancient dwellings in the forest near Sedona.

"What I really do mind is when they mess around ancient dwellings by planting crystals and burning candles in the walls, playing their spiritual games. The Forest Service also doesn't much care to have thousands of these New Age worshipers show up—like during that Harmonic Convergence thing back in the late 1980s. What a conglomeration! All of them humming to bring the earth into a higher vibration level. Yeah...right!

"But this land is fragile, you know? It can't hold thousands of people trampling over it, squatting to do their business behind every other bush. What angered me were not so much the worshipers, but the nuts that came along with them, scrounging around, making money off such an event. As God is in His heaven, I tell you there was even one guy trying to sell tickets to ride a UFO.

"Sedona sure can attract some nuts, some real off-the-wall people who think this place is sacred, whatever 'sacred' means. Frankly, I think the word 'sacred' is used to sell lectures, crystals, psychic readings and Jeep tour rides. I've lived here all my life and Sedona has changed from a nice rural community to one that's fake. Yeah, that's right. Sedona is a fake city, built on tourism, New Age cults, and fancy houses with guard gates. Well, if it's so sacred, I sure haven't seen these people treat this land in a sacred way, considering all the trash I've picked up!" He hitches up his gun belt again. Clearly, there is anger in his voice.

Joel Miller's time with the Forest Service is almost over. Next month, he'll retire with 38 years to his credit.

"Yeah. I've done 38 years. I started with the Forest Service when I was just 20 years old. Sounds like a prison sentence, huh? But it hasn't been. I don't mean it to sound like that. I've had my ups and downs like anybody has with a job that's lasted this long. It becomes routine.

"But the one thing I can say is that I really care about this land. I've been her protector for 38 years, but I've seen things that make me wonder if the earth is worth saving for humans. Sometimes, I think it would be better if we started this human race thing all over again, with a new slate, you know?"

He thinks about that statement for a moment and his eyes gleam a little in the setting sun. "Yeah, a new slate."

Joel and his wife, Margie, plan to move to their ranch in Wyoming, where Joel's been planting acres of Christmas trees during the past few years whenever he could get time off from his job.

Joel takes a parting glace at the beautiful city below him and heads toward his green Forest Service vehicle where he pulls the chewed cigar out of his mouth and sticks it in his pocket, careful not to drop anything on the ground.

"Yes, Sedona is beautiful in its way, but I'm going someplace where it's green all year long. I've seen quite enough of these red rocks...and the people that go with them."

CHAPTER 22

The sound of her own scream jolted Kathleen awake. She lay in her bed, shaking, afraid to move because the terrifying nightmare still flooded over her.

Since Scott died, she found herself reliving her life with him in her dreams. They always seemed to resemble a rat maze where she could find no way out, and when she did, her priest, Father O'Malley, stood blocking her access to a new life.

But this night's dream was different, and far more frightening. In it, she had walked into a Sedona tourist shop, one of the dozens of places that sell cheap items to bring home to the kids or granny—funky key rings, a tarantula or scorpion buried in a mound of plastic, or fanny packs with Cathedral Rock emblazoned in sienna.

On the wall, toward the back of the shop was a peculiar hanging, a pentagram-shaped object with feathers, crystals, and New Age dream keepers attached to it. As Kathleen turned to ask the owner about the hanging, she saw Scott standing in a corner eyeing her. His face was the same, but he was changed somehow. Trying to discern the difference, she suddenly realized Scott's ears were pointed and small, and sharp horns grew from his forehead. Although his body was that of a man, his legs were that of a goat.

In horror, she realized Scott had taken the form of a satyr, the lecherous half-man, half-animal from Greek mythology. She tried to run from him, but he was faster than she, and he knocked her down with his hoofs. As he mounted her, she woke to the sound of her scream.

A cold sweat bathed her body, and she felt pain again in her left clavicle. In desperation to force herself out of the nightmare, she reached over, found the lamp next to her bed and turned on the switch.

The light flooded her bedroom and she sat up, shivering from the cold morning. Beside the bed was the new Bible Richard gave her for her birthday.

As a Roman Catholic, Kathleen always read her St. Joseph Sunday Missal which included portions of the New Testament. But during her discussions with Richard about the teachings of Christ, Kathleen realized she knew little of the Bible. She was delighted with the gift not only because she was interested in the historical significance of the book, but she also wanted to understand Richard's faith. To her surprise, she found the writing lyrical. The more she read, the more she wondered how she, as a writer, had ignored reading a book of such magnitude.

Still experiencing the ravages of her nightmare, Kathleen picked up the Bible and flipped randomly through the pages, ending up in Proverbs. One sentence stood out as she began to read:

"The fear of the Lord is the beginning of knowledge,
But fools despise wisdom and instruction." Proverbs 1:7

Kathleen tried to absorb what she just read. She never feared the Lord, not even when she walked into the confessional. She felt more fear of the priest than God. It was the priest who sat in judgment of her, not God, not the God who hung in effigy over the altar. That God was too far removed from her consciousness because the hierarchy of the Roman Catholic Church stood between. God was a distant deity to Kathleen, one to be placated at the confessional and afterward with penance, but not to be thought of personally through fear or love.

She continued to read, interested in the instructional nature of Proverbs but soon came upon words that caused her to gasp.

"Whoever commits adultery with a woman lacks understanding;
He who does so destroys his own soul." Proverbs 6:32

She reread the passage and the words swam before her eyes. Even though she did not think of herself as an adulteress, her love affair with Richard suddenly took on another tone.

She slammed the book shut. Was it not different because they had fallen in love with one another? The love between them was not just physical, it had become an emotional and spiritual attachment. She now saw him every day, made love with him, cooked his dinners, washed his clothes, and they spoke wondrously of the oneness of their souls.

Although he did not live with her, in every other way, he was like her husband, soothing her, caressing her, sharing himself, his thoughts with her, even his born-again Christian beliefs, which she was struggling to understand.

Would he lose his soul because of her, as he had said weeks ago?

Kathleen sat up in bed, hugging the Bible to her until she dozed off. When she woke, the sun was beginning to soften the darkness of the night. She heard Richard unlock the door and he came to her bed.

He kissed her, running his finger over the features of her face, but she did not, could not, respond to his attentions after the lessons of the night. Instead, she stiffened.

"What is it? What's wrong?" There was concern in his voice because she would not look at him. "Kathleen, Kathleen! Talk to me, what is it?"

Finally, he took her chin in his hand and turned her face to him. "Look at me. If I'm going to burn in hell, I want all of you. Don't separate yourself from me like this."

"Oh, God! You do believe that, don't you?" she cried out.

He did not answer, but just continued to hold her face in his hands, looking into her terrified eyes.

"I read some of Proverbs, the sixth chapter. It says that when a man commits adultery, he loses his soul. Oh, Richard!" She grabbed him, hugging him tightly.

The silence grew between them. They both knew the answer to their dilemma but each was afraid to speak, knowing the words would become reality.

Instead, he stroked her hair, her face. "Why didn't I always have you?" he asked aloud, but seemed to speak to himself.

She hid her face in his shoulder.

"Kathleen, listen to me. You're not a seductress. You didn't lure me here. I am at fault, not you. You told me to think about what I was doing and I did. I am the one who has given my life to the Lord. It is I who have done the sinning. I hadn't considered how deeply I would fall in love with you."

She pulled away from him. There was anger in her voice, anger at God.

"I've waited all my life to find you and now that I have, I'm damned for it! How could your merciful Jesus Christ do this to me? I've been a good, faithful woman, trying to act morally, responsibly. If this life is like what the New Agers say, a lesson, I'm tired of lessons. I want more. I want you!"

She stopped. The truth had slipped out of her mouth.

She saw a flicker of anger in his eyes when she mentioned New Agers, but instead he softly touched her face. "I wanted to tell you earlier in the week, but I couldn't—I'm going home this weekend. It's my daughter's birthday."

She took a deep breath. "It would be better if you told me you were leaving me. Every day, you know, I wait for you to do it. Why don't you just do it and get it over with?"

He smiled for the first time. "You'll have to get rid of me."

"And what if I can't?"

He avoided her question. "Listen, I love you, Kathleen, don't you know that? I think my wife knows something has happened. She must sense there's a difference when I talk to her on the phone. I've changed. I know now what it's like to feel the kind of love I've dreamed of all my life. I'll not give it up easily. My wife and I, we've had a good marriage. It has been loving, all that I could ask for then. But with you, it's different. I feel like I'm living again, not existing."

"I don't want you to go," Kathleen said. Her voice sounded like a petulant teenager.

He lovingly stroked her hair. "I know...I know. Just keep this in your heart my dearest Kathleen: You're the love of my life. I don't have anything else to give you but that."

Chapter 23

MEMO

To: Kathleen Sullivan
From: Jack Berens
Subject: Real estate agents

Sedona's real estate is skyrocketing, and it seems like there's a real estate office on every corner. I hear there's several hundred real estate agents jockeying for sales in Sedona alone, marketing every damn piece of ground they can get their hands on. What's it like to be a real estate agent in Sedona? Get hold of one of those top sales agents. I'd like to know their game.

George Mason
"It's the View"
By Kathleen Sullivan
The *Sedona Chronicle*

G eorge Mason's wide smile shows brilliant white teeth. After all, today is another day he hopes to make a bundle of money by selling the red rocks of Sedona. It's also another day that he can sell the Lord to prospective clients of heaven.

"I just know this lovely couple coming my way will do me and the Lord justice," George says. He brushes the dandruff off his coat and straightens the small gold cross he wears as a tie tack.

George, a short man with a close-cut haircut, extends his small manicured hand toward the husband and nods his head at the wife. A man who likes order above all else, George is meticulous about his clothing. Not one spot can be seen on his expensive coat and slacks, his highly polished Italian loafers. For George, a wrinkled collar would simply be out of the question.

"Howdy, folks. I'm George Mason. I understand from my broker that you're interested in purchasing a home here in this beautiful red rock country. My, my! You just couldn't have picked a nicer day to find that home. Isn't it simply gorgeous out?" He wipes his forehead nervously with his silk handkerchief.

The couple smile in tandem. Henry and Harriet Lewis, a couple in their early 60s, call Seattle home, but they've made enough money through the years and now want a second home amid the beauty of Sedona.

"This is our second time here, George, and we just love it! I can't tell you how thrilled we are to even be discussing the possibility of finding a new home with you as our guide! We understand from your broker that you're one of the top real estate salesmen in Sedona," Harriet says with fervor.

She pokes Henry in the side. "Well, say something, Henry!"

"Yes, what Mother says is true," Henry says, referring to his large, hulking wife. Harriet is dressed in a large, Hawaiian muumuu, a style that does not fit Sedona's western casualness. She's busy fanning herself with a real estate magazine that shows many of the properties for sale in the area.

George Mason is an old hand at helping people pick out their dream home. He's been doing it for 15 years, beginning when Sedona was on the cusp of the real estate boom. By the time the boom really hit the community in the late 1980s, Mason was selling houses and God at an alarming rate of three houses a month and two conversions a week.

Although the recession of the early 1990s enveloped Sedona's real estate market just like any other area of the United States, George always makes sales when other Realtors are sitting high and dry. He credits his sales record to the Lord.

"Why, the beauty of Sedona was what drew me to this blessed area those many years ago, and it was then that the Lord told me my calling was to help people find their dream home. It's the Lord that gives me this special talent, the Lord! He is next to my side every day and gives me that blessed intuition to lead these wonderful people who flock here—like the Lewis'—to their new home."

Along with the ability to close a deal like a steel trap—be it a small trailer next to Oak Creek or a mansion in the Soldier Pass area—George also sees to it that he gives witness about the Lord in the process.

But that's not done until the sale is clinched tighter than a cinch on a bucking bronco. George says sometimes people get offended with his witnessing while he's trying to close the deal. Once he's got the home buyers hooked and money plunked down to start escrow, it's then that he gives a rah rah boost for the Lord.

"Why, this is the Lord's country here. You can just see these rocks are carved by the hand of the Lord. What better job could I have than selling these wonderful people a piece of this red land that the Lord took a personal interest in!"

While Henry and Harriet Lewis take turns using the rest room at the real estate office, George says confidentially, "It's just so exhilarating to witness to folks about the Lord, particularly after they hand me a nice, juicy check. Praise the Lord!"

After a quiet talk about how much money Henry and Harriet want to pay for their dream home, how many bedrooms, baths and other amenities they are looking for, George plows into the listings, coming up with three possible homes the couple might like.

George is quite heartened by their likes and dislikes—and the money they want to spend—between $400,000 to $450,000. They also look like a couple who would take his preaching and not be offended, he says in a quiet aside as they all walk toward George's new white Cadillac Seville.

The first house on George's list is off Dry Creek Road. Located in an area with a security gate, it has a southwestern look with adobe walls and a red tiled roof. After a walk through the four bedroom, three bath home, Harriet says, "It's pretty, George. I'll grant you that. But the view is too far away, too distant. It's a beautiful view, but not the right view."

Never one to argue with a client about the Lord's handiwork, George takes them to a home in the Soldier Pass area that is completely surrounded by junipers and pinon pines.

"Look at this deck! It sits out over the wash and in the winter and spring, you can hear the water flow. This house was designed by one of the area's leading architects and has three levels. One for entertaining, one for complete privacy and the other for family activities. I think this would suit you very well."

Harriet disagrees, thumping her fat fingers on her oversized black purse. "It's a gracious home, I'll grant you that, George. But I can't see the red rocks at all from here. Whoever designed this didn't understand people come here to see the red rocks."

The last house is located off Verde Valley School Road, past the Village of Oak Creek. This house is also in a secluded subdivision, and has a New Mexico feel to it, with a large sunken front room, and a fireplace that resembles a pueblo outdoor oven. Glass surrounds the house on all sides, and the view of the red rocks is spectacular, almost as if one could touch them from any area of the house.

Harriet drags Henry, a man about half her size, throughout the house, murmuring oh's and ah's at each corner, each cupboard, each view. Henry nods while Harriet pulls out the checkbook.

"How much is the house, George?"

"Well, it's a little over what you said you want to pay. It's $510,000, but there is the possibility that the owner would be willing to accept a lesser amount." George eyes the checkbook and pulls out his silk handkerchief again to wipe his brow.

"That's fine. Will a check for $510,000 cover it all or do I need to give a little extra for the escrow costs?"

George gives a nervous laugh. "My goodness, Mrs. Lewis! You really only need give me a small amount to hold the house while it goes through escrow."

"Well, would $200,000 do?"

"Yes, yes. Of course! I suppose you're happy with the view?"

"Most definitely," she says. "The view will help us to focus our concentration. To know all realities and thus attain enlightenment is to know one's own mind, don't you agree, George?"

The Realtor stands mute, not quite grasping Harriet's meaning. She hands George the check. "Yes, this will work out quite well. The silence, the beauty, the rocks. The examination of one's own mind through meditation is the key to knowledge and this place will do that very well for us. You know, George, since all physical objects are merely reflections, like these red rocks here, the inner mind is indeed the only reality."

He looks down at the check Harriet has just handed him and sputters, "Thank the Lord!"

Harriet eyes George in a forceful way. "The Lord has nothing to do with it! All our money comes from teaching enlightenment to those poor souls who flail about as Christians. We teach the true reality, George! We are Ch'an Buddhists."

CHAPTER 24

Philip Buckley was feeling expansive, especially after last night's romp with Elizabeth Ashton. He roamed about the bar at Los Abrigados Resort, greeting people he knew through his brother. It was a task he normally disliked, but today he enjoyed taking Scott's place in Sedona society.

Philip was casually dressed in a white golf shirt and shorts, but it was apparent by the quality of the clothing that the outfit was financially out of reach for the average man. He looked around him. The bar, with its big screen TV and its pretty barmaids drew a large crowd on the weekends. He felt it was a good place to be seen.

"Well, hello, John. I haven't seen you in a while," Philip said to John Talbot who was having a drink at the bar while watching a pro football game.

John was president of Keep Sedona Beautiful, a grass-roots organization that often played a lead role in monitoring development in and around Sedona. Philip knew Talbot needed to be courted if the organization's board of directors were going to support the land exchange that he was working on so diligently.

Talbot shook Philip's hand. "Hello, Philip. I've been meaning to give you a call. I wonder if you would mind meeting with the board fairly soon and outlining what this land exchange deal is supposed to accomplish. All I've heard is the brouhaha from those people out in Edgarville who are calling foul."

Philip ordered his usual gin and tonic and Talbot sipped on a draft beer.

"Good, God, Philip! It didn't help that your sister-in-law did that piece for the *Chronicle* about their concerns. What a group of malcontents, forming their own militia!"

Philip chuckled to himself about how easy his plan was working. He didn't even have to make the suggestion to meet.

"Of course, John, I'd be more than happy to meet with the board. What you need to keep in mind is that Kathleen is painting a lousy picture of this deal because she's no longer a beneficiary of Scott's will. I really think it's sour grapes."

Talbot nodded. "There are others in the community who believe that as well."

Philip was glad to hear that tidbit of information about Kathleen. She stepped into her own trap by writing that alarmist article in that mealy-mouthed little newspaper. He continued his amiable explanation.

"As for the people in Edgarville, well, John, you know the Buckley family has always cared about Sedona. We're pioneers here—well, practically! Nothing will be done without the residents' knowledge, public hearings, all of those processes that make this a democracy, despite what those rabble rousers with their guns believe out there!"

Talbot fingered his beer bottle. "What's really going to happen on that land, Philip?"

"If the trade is approved, I'm working on several proposals for the 100 acres. One of them is a regional airport. I think you'll agree that an airport is needed if this area is to grow wisely. The Sedona airport on the mesa is a hazard, in my view, and I know many Sedona residents are concerned about it being located in the middle of the city."

Talbot agreed. "Yes, there have been complaints about the airport. The city and airport authority are attempting to address those issues. A regional airport near Edgarville would be a relief, but could create other problems.

The land trade is a complex situation, Philip. My group has concerns, and I know you understand that."

He drained the last of his beer. "It's good to see you, Philip. Call my office next week, will you, so we can set up the meeting."

"Be glad to John. We very much want your organization's support."

Philip sipped his drink and thought about the weekend. He had spent the night with Elizabeth Ashton, his brother's whore. It gave him a sense of power to know that not only did he control his brother's money, he also could hump Elizabeth until she screamed for mercy. She never would let him near her while Scott was alive, but now that the bastard was dead, she was offering herself to him in as many ways as he could conjure up.

In Philip's mind, political power, monetary power, and sexual power were all the same: it was manipulation, plain and simple.

That thought reminded Philip of his morning golf game at Sedona Golf Resort with some of Scott's cronies, men whose money quietly controlled Sedona. Philip arranged the game because he felt he needed to smooth over the nasty business of the court ruling Scott an alcoholic.

Sedona Golf Resort, with its emerald green course set against the rust-colored rock monoliths, was a perfect place to continue his scheme. Considered one of the most beautiful golf resorts in Arizona, Philip was indifferent to the scenery as he played golf with Scott's friends. He had other work to do.

Lawrence Emerson, owner of a resort in Oak Creek Canyon, just shot an eagle on the tenth hole, and looked hard at Philip whose play was ragged. There was a note of disrespect in his voice.

"You don't play often do you, Philip? My personal philosophy is that's a sure sign of a man who only cares about making money, not about being part of the community like your brother Scott."

Philip was prepared for Emerson's antagonism. "That's true, Larry. I'm the one who ran the majority of the business, allowing Scott to have his other pleasures."

The tone in Emerson's voice did not change despite his knowing that Philip had just taken the offensive. "I'm interested to know, Philip, just how you intend to pull off getting a regional airport approved for that acreage over near Edgarville. I've talked to members of the county board of supervisors, and they're not amenable to your plan."

"I know that, Larry. In fact, I've also been in contact with the supervisors. I know they're not warm to the idea. But that's just one of the possibilities for the land. I have several other irons in the fire."

Suddenly, there was less disrespect in Emerson's voice. "Really? Anything I could get involved with? Financially, I mean."

Philip looked up from his putt and smiled knowingly at his golf partner. For once, his ball moved smoothly into the hole.

"I understand, Larry, from mutual friends—you know how news makes the rounds—that your stock portfolio has taken a sharp dip in recent weeks. You should be thinking about diversifying some of your financial holdings. This land deal could be the solution for you."

Emerson looked shaken but did not reply.

Philip lied easily to Scott's friends, just as he lied to his nieces. The regional airport story was a convenient cover-up until the real deal was cinched. Because of the project's high government priority, no one of any consequence in the government would pay attention to the squawking environmentalists and cantankerous residents of Edgarville. Philip took pride in sending out conflicting stories to keep everyone off balance.

Another one of Scott's friends approached Philip and Larry after making a bogie on the hole. Harold Winn, president of the Sedona-Oak Creek Bank, jammed his putter into his golf bag, angry at his performance.

Winn picked up on the conversation. "Frankly, I think you're sniffing up the wrong tree with a regional airport. A beautiful housing development would go great out there despite those Edgarville kooks, and my bank would love to finance it."

The threesome walked to the next tee.

"When I've got more information in hand, I'll give you both a chance to get involved." Philip's voice was smooth, convincing.

Winn was apprehensive. "But isn't the Forest Service interested in what will be put on that land after they trade it with you?"

"Well, you know how it is with the federal government. The feds want the property in Oak Creek Canyon so bad they can taste it. That's prime riparian habitat. When I talk to those bureaucratic bastards, I can almost hear them slavering over it. The Forest Service isn't much concerned about what goes on that miserable 100 acres near Edgarville."

Emerson interrupted the conversation. "Speaking about the government—I had lunch with the governor last week. You know Judge Kenneth Oswald, don't you, Philip?"

"Slightly," Philip said, not looking directly at Larry Emerson.

"The governor told me word is coming down that the President is going to make an announcement next week, appointing Oswald to the federal bench for this district. Wasn't Oswald the judge who handled Scott's will?"

"Yes, he was," Philip said, " and he handled that distressing business with great compassion. Well, that is good news—my, my a federal judgeship!"

Philip pulled out his expensive Ping driver, acting preoccupied as he got ready to hit the ball. News spreads quickly in this state, Philip thought while he took a practice swing.

He smiled at the sound of a solid hit and watched it sail through the sky, touching the edge of the eleventh green.

Philip enjoyed the power of paying off a favor, even if it did take thousands of dollars in donations to the money-hungry politicians. He knew Oswald's appointment to the federal bench would reap rewards to the Buckleys for years to come.

Philip's thoughts moved away from the golf game to the cool-tasting gin and tonic that flowed down his throat. He eyed the nicely shaped legs of one of the bar maids working the bar.

The appointment of Oswald to the federal bench couldn't have come at a better time. Philip knew his plans were beginning to fall into place.

Chapter 25

MEMO

To: Kathleen Sullivan
From: Jack Berens
Subject: Psychics

I got a call from some God-fearing old lady the other day who complained about the number of so-called psychics operating in every nook and cranny of Sedona. She criticized the New Agers and their proliferation of psychic fairs, saying the devil is enveloping Sedona, an interesting concept but about as far off the wall as the New Agers and their medicine wheels.

How about a story on one of these so-called psychics? What kind of babble do they throw out at one of their readings, and what kind of person chucks away good money to hear their bullshit?

Sal Morton and Brigid Barnes
"I See A Lot of Clarity"
By Kathleen Sullivan
The *Sedona Chronicle*

Brigid Barnes laughs like a schoolgirl when Sal Morton takes her hand and closes his eyes. Even though she sounds like a schoolgirl, Brigid is 39 and feels like she needs some answers about the direction of her life.

"I've never done anything like this before," she tells the psychic.

"I know," he says knowingly.

The two are sitting on the porch of a New Age store in Sedona. The shade of a large sycamore tree brings a feeling of enclosure to the area despite the roar of traffic nearby. Tourists stroll down the sidewalk, passing in and out of various shops and art galleries. No one pays any attention to the two on the porch.

Brigid says she decided yesterday to see a psychic. Although she has lived in Sedona for several years, she's not paid much attention to the New Agers, the psychics, the Jeep tours, the traffic, the tourists, or her personal life.

She says she has holed herself up in her small studio and painted vibrant abstracts of Sedona's monoliths.

In the beginning, she sold her work at local artist fairs and then to a gallery in Jerome. She was able to make ends meet, she says, but the past six months has been difficult financially. None of her abstracts have attracted buyers.

"I feel like my energy is gone from here," she tells Sal. "It's even more difficult—painful even—when I see other artists who aren't as good as I am getting paid thousands of dollars for their work."

Sal nods. His eyes are closed.

Brigid tells Sal he doesn't looks much like a psychic. In her imagination, she says, he should be dressed in a long, flowing garment. Instead, he's dressed in a blue shirt that hangs outside his baggy pants. Sandals adorn his feet, and he wears his brown hair cut short.

"But I like your voice, which is deep, and somehow comforting."

He nods again and Brigid continues to chatter.

During the past several months, Brigid says she has had an urge to stop doing her abstracts. She has had visions of working with Navajo children on the reservation north of Sedona, teaching them to paint their stark surroundings.

"But I've ignored my feelings. That's why I've come to you. I just don't know what to do. This vision is obstructing my creative process."

He is quiet, still holding her hands with his eyes closed. Her fingernails are cut short, but even so, there is paint under the rims, mostly the color of sienna, like the Sedona landscape.

"I'm going to give you some general feelings that I have about you, and then I will answer your question," Sal says finally.

Brigid nods.

"I feel that you are tuned into your higher self and follow your higher self. You move with it and go with it, something that you have always done, like when you picked up and moved to Sedona from...Colorado, yes I feel energy coming from the north, Colorado."

Brigid gasps. "Yes, I'm from Denver!"

"You are also intuitive about people. You can turn into their auric fields and you listen to that intuition."

Brigid sits, fascinated.

Sal continues, "You are very connected to the angelic realm. There are many different realms but you are connected to the angels, the whole routine," Sal says, rushing on, his eyes still closed. He waves his hand in midair to explain his vision.

"I see that there was a major energy shift in your life about three years ago. That was when you decided to move from Denver and come to Sedona."

"Yes!"

"I feel you work your energy through your touch. Some people would call that healing, but you can call it anything you like. I have the feeling that you have the great desire to hug me," he said, opening his eyes and smiling at her.

Brigid laughs, embarrassed. She brushes a dark curl that has dropped onto her forehead, but then sits quietly to hear more.

"I feel that you are here on this earth to change people, but if they are not ready to change, you don't force the issue. You have a very open heart but you are not sucked into this victim stuff. Basically, you know who you are and what you are doing. The energy field around you is very clear. You have your own mission. What I'm talking about is the spiritual field, but that falls over into the physical."

Brigid shifts in her chair.

"About my question..."

"I feel that you are at a spot that is pretty clear, but you are afraid to go forward. But what I see is that there is so much clarity around you. It's like jumping off a bridge, something like that, and you will be protected. You can go forward with your life and know you will be protected. I see a strong masculine being around you. He is not of the angelic realm. I see him as a shaft of light, blue light. He is far removed from this duality, but he is your main guide telling you, 'This is what you need to do. Get off the stick and go for it.'"

He continues. "You need to take the chance and do this. Trust yourself and go with it. I see a lot of clarity there. Your guidance is all around you and will always be there for you."

Sal is silent for about three minutes. His eyes are still closed. Brigid has shifted a little in her chair but remains focused on Sal.

"What I have to tell you is very important," Sal says. "I feel this as it's coming to me. What you need to do is get centered within yourself. It's like falling down a shaft. You won't touch bottom, but as soon as you center yourself, there will be a door and you will step through it. You will leave behind all the rules and regulations that you have been equipped with all of your life, but everything will be OK once you center yourself."

Sal opened his eyes and looks at her. He nods. "I don't know what that means, but maybe you will someday."

Brigid sits quietly for a few moments, trying to absorb what Sal has just told her. Her eyes are not focused on anything in particular because she is in deep thought. The traffic roars by, but Brigid hears nothing. Sal sits quietly, understanding Brigid's thoughts.

Suddenly, she looks up and smiles at the psychic, reaches in her jeans and pulls out a $20 bill, money she really can't afford.

"Thanks," she says. "You've just confirmed what I've known for months. I need to leave this place."

CHAPTER 26

The deep blue water in Montezuma Well glistened in the late afternoon sunlight, drawing Kathleen closer to the edge of the limestone sink. Along with the extraordinary color of the water, she noticed a scum-like algae floating around the sink's edge with scores of turtles snapping at insects on the water's surface.

Formed long ago by the collapse of an immense underground cavern, Montezuma Well is a national monument about 20 miles southeast of Sedona and off the beaten track, attracting fewer tourists than other scenic areas surrounding the tourist city. Its fresh water spring feeds the sink continuously with crystal-clear water, the same water used centuries ago by the ancient Sinagua Indians to irrigate their crops of maize and squash.

This late in the afternoon, Kathleen was the only person at the well. It was quiet, except for the soft sound of the wind rustling through the Indian ruins built below the rim of the sink.

Putting on a pair of tennis shoes she always carried in the trunk of her car, Kathleen hiked down the trail and sat near the ruins which were marked with graffiti from pioneers who passed through the area a century ago.

Everyone wants their name in print, she thought ruefully, looking at the hundred-year-old signatures and dates scarring the dwellings of the ancient Sinagua.

She wondered about the daily lives of those long-ago natives. Did people feel love as she and Richard, or was mating done simply as a matter of procreation and survival of the species? She felt that life was probably easier if love wasn't involved.

Kathleen's contemplation turned to the Bible and she remembered that it spoke beautifully of the love between a man and a woman. In fact, the Bible spoke not only of love, but of every other human obsession—lust, hate, fear, murder, homosexuality, avarice, and corruption. It occurred to her that human behavior hadn't changed much through the centuries.

Kathleen knew she had made a fool of herself after that horrifying nightmare. She had only made the situation between her and Richard more difficult by blurting out her feelings without thinking of the consequences. As a result, Richard came back to Sedona in a subdued mood from his weekend visit with his family. Although Kathleen expected that, she was also hurt by it.

On Monday morning, he came in as usual to have breakfast with her, but he was silent at the kitchen table.

Kathleen touched his hand, her voice filled with concern. "Are you OK?"

He looked at her. Sadness filled his green eyes. "No, I'm not OK, Kathleen. I feel so guilty, so awful. I couldn't look at my wife. I couldn't touch her. She asked me if something was wrong, but I just said the work here was going badly."

Kathleen did not know how to respond. The sin of their love affair was beginning to flood her soul. She alternated between feeling strong enough to let him go and weak enough to beg him to stay. The conflicting feelings caused her to constantly push her emotions down into the well of her being, but she was beginning to show unusual strain. She felt as if she were drowning, often catching herself crying at the most unexpected moments.

She couldn't believe she would cry over such trifling matters as mail still addressed to Mrs. Scott Buckley or while watching a sad story on the evening news. The resolve she made at Scott's funeral to never cry like that again vanished along with a perception that her physical health was changing. She simply did not feel well, but Kathleen was wise enough to know her physical health was finely tuned to her conflicting emotions.

The pain of the affair, and other unresolved issues in her life were inundating her. She felt as if she did not know herself at all anymore, and she was increasingly bothered by her unrelenting hatred of Scott which she considered a mortal sin. The need to return to her faith was constantly on her mind, but she feared the confessional worse than she feared hell.

Needing to get away from Sedona for a few hours, Kathleen drove to Montezuma Well to think. She picked up a stone and threw it into the limestone sink, watching the turtles scatter.

Kathleen saw the natural beauty around her, but felt the sharp stab of loneliness.

She thought about Richard as she walked along the trail, around and up from the back of the well. There she found a steep stairway, climbed down it and followed a trail along an irrigation ditch, used eons ago by the Sinagua.

Finally, she came to a large sycamore tree, its trunk stretching out from the side of the hill, its roots feeding at the heart of the spring that flowed into the limestone sink.

Her love affair with Richard was wrong, dead wrong, she realized as she sat beneath the sycamore, its leaves yellow and brittle, falling softly in the November wind. No sweet words about the love between them could soften the hardness of the wrong being done—against God, against Richard's wife, and the ultimate spiritual and emotional harm to both herself and Richard.

The affair was wrong not just for religious reasons, but because Kathleen knew it was antithesis to herself, her ethical structure so tightly woven from her Irish background.

If she could let him go, she thought, then the cloud of sin would lift from her and she would be able to function again, to live again even though she knew she would long desperately for him.

She rubbed her hand over the base of the large sycamore, feeling the names of past sweethearts who carved their love for one another in the tree. Kathleen left the spring wondering how she would tell Richard it was over.

Kathleen stood at her kitchen sink washing dishes from breakfast. Although she felt calm on her drive home from the well, Kathleen became tearful once she came home to the surroundings of her life with Richard, to the smell of him in the house.

He came in through the back door, but she did not turn as he set his keys on the kitchen counter, trying to pull herself together. Sensing something wrong, he came up behind her and put his hands on her shoulders.

The act, one of love and concern on his part, caused her to begin sobbing.

Turning around, she cried, "I can't do this any longer Richard! I just can't!"

He stood mute for a moment and then asked her, "Is there something I've done, something I've said?"

Kathleen, choked with tears, could not answer. She wiped her hands on a towel and looked at him through red eyes.

He took her hand and led her to the living room couch. "We need to talk."

She nodded, unable to speak for a moment, then she said, "I'm angry at you."

She pursed her lips together in an effort not to cry. Although she wanted to talk to him desperately about the sin they created together, about her fear of asking God for forgiveness, she could not. So she spoke of the other side of her anger, the reality of his choosing his wife over her.

"I'm angry at you that you could keep your wife and not me."

"I never said that." His voice was sad.

"But I know that."

He sat silently for a while, looking at his hands, soiled with Sedona's red dirt. "It's come down to divorcing her or leaving you. I'm so depressed, I really don't know what I'm doing. My work on the job is suffering. My wife is bewildered, but I didn't tell her about us, I couldn't bring myself to do it."

"Don't you know that I want you to divorce her and marry me?" The words, unaccounted for in her brain, were coming out all wrong, but she could not stop herself. She felt like a train with no brakes, skidding on the tracks as the curve of lost love loomed ahead.

Richard showed surprise at her comment. "You've never made any kind of hint, never pressured me."

"Rarely in my life have I asked for anything for myself. But I love you so much, I have to say it. I just can't believe I will go through my life without you."

He was silent and then said, "But Kathleen, there is One who will always be with you."

A flair of anger burst from her. "Stop it! Stop your preaching to me! Jesus Christ won't lie in my bed with me or sit at my table when I eat my dinner alone." Her voice was hard, unrelenting.

"Yes, He will. He's here." Richard tried to counter her rage.

"That's easy enough for you to say. You have her to warm your bed and sit at your table." She spit out the words like venom.

Richard looked down at his soiled hands, but did not answer.

She took a deep breath. "Richard, you said there's nothing wrong with your marriage. Well, there is, or this wouldn't have happened. You have to make some kind of a decision."

He nodded. "I know there's something wrong. It's the empty nest syndrome when most long-term marriages break up. I must be going though mid-life crisis, or something...My hair is gray, my muscles don't work like they used to. I'm on the down side of my life. For a short time, that was all gone with you. But after I went home for my daughter's birthday, I realized other Things—a life of thirty years with someone I can't hurt."

He reached out and took her hand. "I know that you don't like my preaching. I just want to tell you that there is a beautiful passage in the Bible that says, 'Be still and listen to the Lord.'"

God, does he always preach when he can't face something, Kathleen thought angrily. She yanked her hand away from him.

"Well, maybe I did today," she said mocking him and the Lord. "I drove to Montezuma Well and thought about us and how wrong this whole thing is."

She began crying again. "We have to end it. No more, Richard. No more."

No more love in the afternoon or walks in the evening watching the sun's last rays kiss the red rocks goodnight. No more feeling like someone loves me, she thought with a terrible dread that filled her whole being.

He sat crying with her for a long time. Finally, he got up to leave and she cried out, "Richard, please bring me the Bible!"

He turned in surprise.

"I want to confess my sins to Jesus and ask for His forgiveness. I want you to be my witness." For the second time, she was astounded by her actions. It was as if she had no control over herself.

He did as she asked, and they clasped hands while Kathleen made her tearful declaration. They sat for a while, silent at the unexpected turn of events. Finally, Richard simply opened the Bible randomly to read to Kathleen, and Hebrews 6:13-20 fell before him.

"He has given us both His promise and His oath. Two things
we can completely count on, for it is impossible for God to tell a
lie. Now all those who flee to him to save them can take new
courage when they hear such assurances from God; now they
can know without doubt that he will give them the salvation He
has promised them."

His voice was filled with gladness. "How appropriate! It's as if the Lord knows what we are going through, and this is His reassurance."

Richard lifted his face from the Bible and fell to his knees asking aloud forgiveness for his sins. Then he said, "Lord, I love this woman. Protect and care for her. Forgive us both for this forbidden love we have shared."

He got up, turned, pulled Kathleen to her feet, and kissed her, full and hard on the mouth. Richard picked up his keys and walked out the door. She could hear his car drive away, and then there was nothing.

She sat still in the growing darkness for a long time, thinking. What had she done, Kathleen asked herself, angrily.

She made it effortless for Richard to leave her by taking on the mantle of a born-again Christian, half because of her guilt, half of her doing it to please him. Why did she always have to please the men in her life, always doing what they wanted because she needed their love?

Kathleen no more believed her sins were gone because of her unthinking declaration than she believed in the babble of the New Agers. For Kathleen, the only spiritual cleansing she knew was facing God through Father O'Malley.

And she didn't have enough courage to do that.

CHAPTER 27

MEMO

To: Kathleen Sullivan
From: Jack Berens
Subject: The rich and famous

It's time to talk to one of Sedona's rich and famous. How about setting up an interview with that gal, Norma Hopkins, whose been an actress on Broadway for so many years? I hear she's a real firebrand who thinks Sedona should be a community only for the rich, an interesting thought. I wonder how all these rich people would live without the poor working class doing their grunt work for them.

Norma Hopkins
"Let Them Eat Cake"
By Kathleen Sullivan
The *Sedona Chronicle*

The mornings are chilly now as late fall sprinkles frost atop the red crags of Sedona, but Norma Hopkins, the famous Broadway actress, can still be seen briskly walking her dog, Johnny.

Although the crime rate in Sedona is low, the large male Rottweiler gives Norma a sense of security as she trots down Soldiers Pass Road wearing her Russian sable jacket over her expensive jogging suit. A blue silk snood covers her signature flame red hair, yet accents it.

Norma loves Sedona, although New York is still her favorite place to live, high among the skyscrapers in one of those penthouse apartments overlooking Central Park.

Still the star of various Broadway plays after nearly 40 years of sweating under the bright lights, Norma spends what little off time she has in this red rock country.

"I cannot tell you, darling, just how invigorating this wonderful town is! Fine restaurants, wonderful art shows, beautiful galleries, world class chamber music and jazz concerts, and charming local plays. All so very, very delightful! It's like a mini-New York stuck among the red rocks."

Norma is a little breathless from the swift walk. A small line of perspiration gathers on her upper lip, and she wipes it away with a delicate hand, nails flashing scarlet, accented by the large diamond ring given to her by her fifth husband.

"Why just the other day, I had lunch with a delightful group of ladies that meet once a month. We have such fun going to the different restaurants in town. "Let me see, there is Nan, whose husband is a banker here in town; there is Margie who used to design costumes for RKO in its heyday; there is Stella who is so very active with the homeless girls' thrift shop and whose husband was a CEO for one of the Fortune 500; and there is Darlene, who belongs to one of those Granny dancing groups. She used to be a professional dancer when she was younger. We have great fun kidding her about those skimpy costumes she wears! But she has such a sharp figure, I think she should show all she's got while she's got it! In the end, darling, gravity gets us all."

Norma knows how to fight gravity. She takes a brisk walk every morning, spends thirty minutes in her lap pool, then she meets with her masseuse for an hour. Later, she has a delightful herbal toning facial and then a vegetarian lunch.

In the afternoon, she's usually off shopping, visiting or playing bridge with a group of cronies, New Yorkers who flock to Sedona to get away from that state's frigid winter. Sometimes, if the weather's just perfect, she'll play a round of golf or several sets of tennis.

"I think this is the perfect place to live! The weather is just right and there is so much to do here. If I get bored-which I hardly ever do—I can just hop one of those little flights from Sedona to Phoenix and go shopping or lunching there."

While chattering about Sedona, Norma is also trying to rein in Johnny, who is barking at a group of javelina that have wandered near the roadway.

"My, aren't those nasty looking things! Come here Johnny! Stop that!" she calls out with a touch of fright in her voice. The wild animals who resemble pigs hear the dog and the thin collar of white hair on the back of their necks stand up as they run in the opposite direction.

Although there are plenty of large, estate-like homes in the Soldiers Pass area, the javelina, or collared peccary, still roam about, rooting up bulbs and plants, much to the dismay of those who like to garden.

"Why, last evening, just as I was getting ready for bed, I heard coyotes howl near my house. This is so different than hearing the sirens of New York City, I must say!" she says, referring to the wild nature of Sedona.

Norma built her million-dollar home in the Soldiers Pass area about five years ago. She helped design the showplace, which has five bedrooms, a library, a sauna and Jacuzzi, and a lap swimming pool that borders one side of her black marble living room so Norma can swim in any kind of weather. The water from the lap pool falls gently through a magnificent red rock waterfall into an outside pool built on a lower deck of the house.

The actress has always been involved with politics and politicos—two of her five husbands served as advisors to several presidents, and she proudly reels off the names of other statesmen she has known in and out of the bedroom. As a result of her political acumen she has kept a sharp eye on the evolving cityhood of Sedona.

"I think Sedona incorporating as a city a few years ago was the best thing that ever happened to this wonderful place. As a city, we are in charge of our own destiny, we do not have to depend on the county to maintain our roads, build our sewer, or plan how this area will grow," Norma says, enunciating every word as if she were still on the stage.

"This one issue that came up recently, affordable housing is a hot potato, I will tell you! I do not see any reason why the city should get involved in zoning for affordable housing. This is not that kind of place! There is culture and art here, and beauty. People come here for spirituality.

"This place draws hundreds of people who have made their mark on this world—presidents of large corporations, theatrical people, renowned artists, writers, musicians, business people, and heads of large non-profit organizations. These people only want beauty around them, not stilted, poorly designed and managed affordable housing that will be ripped up by the tenants in a few years. Believe me, I have seen affordable housing and its effects in New York, and we do not want that in Sedona!"

Norma finds herself getting upset at the very thought of affordable housing in this red rock country so dear to her heart.

"There are other places in the Verde Valley to live if people cannot afford the prices here. I must say, there certainly are enough mobile home parks in Sedona for poorer people to move into if they want, although I personally think they should be bulldozed to the ground, but city officials don't have enough guts to do that. I do not know why we need any more public discussion of zoning for affordable housing. What affordable housing does is bring down the price of my home and that of my neighbors," she says as she turns back toward her home, jerking Johnny's choke chain.

Is this a case of 'let them eat cake,' like Marie Antoinette said of the peasants of France?

"No," Norma says in a defiant tone as she walks up her steps where large pots are planted with winter blooming pansies and stock. She yanks again on Johnny's choke chain because he wants to stop and leave his mark on the pots.

She pulls down her snood and unzips her fur jacket before opening the door of her home, giving a look that only a renowned Broadway actress would know how to throw at an out-of-favor critic as she leaves the stage.

"Personally, I think Marie was misquoted by some nasty reporter, such as yourself. As for myself, I can speak freely, not because I am a celebrity, although that does help because the press loves to report on my every word, but because I am an active, well-informed citizen of this community. The point, my dear, is that I may be a fake redhead, but underneath, I am no blond bimbo!"

Chapter 28

Tired from a hard day of work at the newspaper, Kathleen decided when she arrived home that she needed to take a walk to clear her head.

Working at the *Chronicle* was becoming more difficult by the day, she realized as she changed her clothes. Several weeks ago she overheard Jack speaking on the telephone to the owner of the company in Cottonwood where the paper was printed, apologizing because his check bounced.

When Jack got off the phone, his face was red from embarrassment. He looked over at Lauren and Kathleen, and said in an offhand manner, "The press run is going to be cut by several thousand newspapers from now on."

Lauren looked at him in astonishment. "You mean the extra newspapers that are distributed to the hotels, motels, and restaurants?"

"Yes, that's where the cut will be." His answer was curt.

"You're kidding, Jack. Cutting the press run is a disastrous move. It's the tourists who frequent the majority of our advertisers, not your subscribers."

"Maybe so, but the *Chronicle's* subscribers are its foundation in the community. That foundation will keep this paper going in the future," he answered stubbornly.

Lauren's prediction proved right. Those businesses catering to the tourist industry canceled their ads because of the smaller press run. As a result, Jack asked Kathleen and Lauren not to cash their paychecks until he could get money into the bank.

Heeding an internal warning, Kathleen called her mother before she left for work. The conversation included her problems at the newspaper.

"You know, Kathleen, why don't you come back to Los Angeles?" her mother said. "You could live with me until you find a job and a place of your own. You sound so unhappy, I'm afraid your decision to move back to Sedona was a wrong one."

Kathleen was silent for a moment, thinking. "I think you're right, Mom. I'll work on my resume and start sending it to papers in Southern California. Maybe I could even find a position again at the *Times*."

Depression clouded her mind since Richard left almost two weeks ago. She alternated between a feeling of freedom from the affair and despair because it had ended. Her emotions came to the surface once again after she interviewed Norma Hopkins and began walking toward her car. The actress's home and social life reminded Kathleen of her life with Scott and suddenly she began crying. She cried a long time in the safe confines of her car, but looked pale by the time she arrived back at the newspaper.

"God, Kathleen! Is something the matter?" Lauren asked when she saw Kathleen.

"Everything, Lauren. Just everything," Kathleen answered her co-worker. She was afraid to look directly at Lauren for fear she would begin weeping again.

With the problems at work and her emotional state of mind, Kathleen turned to sleep as an escape, seeking her bed almost as soon as she came home in the evening, but found herself wide awake every night as the clock struck 1 a.m. She was tempted to begin using an over-the-counter sleeping pill to help her get through the night, but a nagging feeling about her health forced her to drink herbal tea instead. The tea helped her sleep, but the mornings always seemed so bleak; she had to face another day without Richard.

Today, Kathleen told herself she needed to get some exercise, recognizing the symptoms of her depression. She began walking up Andante Drive toward the water tower just as the late autumn sun began to set.

The spread of the sun's golden glow made the features of the red rocks stand out clearly against the green of the pinon pines and junipers. The scene looked like one from a post card, Kathleen thought as she walked closer to the red rock formations.

The air was brisk and Kathleen could see her own breath as she puffed her way up the street. All around were signs of winter's approach. Fruit trees were nearly bare of leaves and vegetable gardens lay fallow. Some homeowners along the street were beginning to decorate for the Christmas holidays by putting up strings of lights along the front of their mobile homes.

When she got to the top of Andante Drive, to where the water tank stood in its dull glory, she stopped and looked up at Capital Butte. To the west, the sky projected colors of orange, magenta, and pink caught in the indigo clouds as the sun began its decline. It was a perfect scene for the tourist trying to capture that last shot of Sedona before heading out of town.

Kathleen leaned up against the fencing that protected the water tank in order to catch her breath. As the twilight deepened, she could make out the line of the red rocks, with the butte resembling the dome of a capitol building, and further north, the rocks gave the perfect outline of a coffee pot.

Was there something spiritual about these rocks as the New Agers believed, she asked herself. Her natural instinct as a skeptical reporter found the notion absurd. For Kathleen, if there was any spirituality to be found among the crags and buttes and canyons, the commercialism of Sedona brought that spirituality down to the basics of human greed.

Kathleen found herself irritated by the New Agers red rock-inspired spirituality, with their multitude of psychics, healers, sessions and seminars, each looking to make their fortune off someone seeking the truth of life. The people she met in the supermarket parking lot singing the praises of pyramid power were a perfect example of P.T. Barnum's 'There's a sucker born every minute' philosophy.

The problem was, as Kathleen saw it, for every true psychic and healer, every seminar and session to help the spiritual find themselves, Sedona also lured the charlatan, the quick buck artist, the soothsayers, the cult leaders who hammered into their followers that theirs was the only true path to enlightenment—all for a stiff price.

It was a story Kathleen saw as one of the most important in Sedona. Yet those who talked to her about it, off the record, were unwilling to provide hard information about the scam artists who penetrated the community, appearing legitimate just because they joined local business or civic organizations.

But Kathleen knew that even if she could prove who those people were, and produce hard evidence in her stories, the pilgrims would still come by the thousands, drawn by national newspaper and magazine articles proclaiming Sedona to be the center for the New Age. They would still climb Bell Rock, seek energy vortexes, buy crystals, meditate in prayer circles, and dole out the cash.

She thought about Scott's daughter, Natalie. Kathleen heard she was a member of a cult located in a commune somewhere off the beaten path among the red rocks. Gossip among the movers and shakers of Sedona said Natalie had turned over her entire inheritance to the cult leader. That didn't surprise Kathleen. All Natalie ever wanted was the love of her father, but he never gave it to her, leaving Natalie to seek comfort in the philosophy of the New Age.

As she began her jog back home in the growing darkness, she thought about the seekers who flock to Sedona. In her way, Kathleen knew she wasn't much different than anyone else in town, seeking a new life in Sedona with Scott those many years ago. And then there was the affair with Richard. What was she seeking then, she asked herself?

When she arrived home, it was dark. As she walked up her driveway, guided by the night light that shined on her back door, she gave a little cry. Richard was sitting on the porch.

Forgetting her vows to keep away from him, she ran into his arms. He hugged her, then he opened the door and they walked into the kitchen where he began to make coffee while she stood against the counter and took in the smell of him again in her home.

"I don't know how I'm going to live my life without you." She knew she had said that to him before, but couldn't help repeating herself.

"It's the same for me, Kathleen. Don't you know that?" he asked.

She nodded. "I don't know anything anymore. I've lost all sense of perspective, of what's right and wrong, of what I want to do with the rest of my life, of my relationship to God. Somehow, even through the nightmare of my marriage to Scott, the facade of it, I had some sense of who I was. Now I have no perspective of that at all."

Suddenly, Richard walked over to her, put his arms around her and began kissing her neck, her face, her lips. Her body reacted to his and she felt the urgency of him against her, knowing what would happen between them. She moved away from him, telling him they couldn't do this, that it was wrong, but he grabbed her by both her arms and pulled her back to him.

"I don't care," he said as he ran his hand between her legs, making her weak with desire.

In a moment, they were together on top of the bed, making love with a passion that neither of them understood. It was as if the sin, now even more forbidden, added to the intensity of the act. Every movement between them was more delicious than the last, bringing them to a climax that left them both gasping.

Neither said a word to the other as they lay spent in each other's arms. Kathleen knew Richard was thinking how easily they both gave up their vows to God. The only answer was to stay away from one another; seeing each other only triggered their passion.

And for Richard, Kathleen understood their sinful act resurrected the duel between his love for God and his love for her. Once again, Richard was caught in the middle.

The telephone rang. Kathleen was reluctant to answer it, knowing if she did the moment between them would be shattered. It continued to ring, and finally in desperation, she got up, grabbed her robe and picked up the damnable instrument.

"Hello?"

"Goodness, Kathleen, I thought you weren't home."

"Well, I am. Who is this?" she asked in an angry tone.

"Oh, I'm sorry! This is Anne Brooks, president of the Sierra Club."

When Kathleen did not respond, Anne kept on.

"I apologize about calling you at home, but I've come across some information I think you really need to know."

"What is it concerning?" Kathleen asked, still irritated by the intrusion.

"Remember that story you did on the land exchange between your late husband's property and the Forest Service property out near Edgarville?"

"Yes."

"Well, I said there was something fishy about that, and you quoted me. Now, I really do think there is something going on."

Suddenly interested, Kathleen said, "Why? In what way?"

Anne said she and other friends who belong to the Sierra Club were hiking around the Edgarville property that morning.

"There were men out there, men doing survey work."

"Well, I don't see anything peculiar about that. Probably the survey work is being done by the Forest Service to mark the boundaries of the property for the exchange."

"No, Kathleen. They weren't with the Forest Service or even hired by the Forest Service because I asked them. In fact, they were acting damn secretive. They wouldn't answer any other questions, but just continued to work as if we weren't there."

Kathleen looked up from the telephone and saw Richard standing near her, dressed.

"Can you hold on a minute, Anne?"

To Richard, she whispered: "Are you leaving?"

"Yes, but I'll see you tomorrow. OK?" His voice sounded tentative, uncertain.

She tried to discern his facial expression, but it was blank. What was he feeling, she wondered after such a forbidden interlude?

"OK," she waved to him, disappointed he couldn't stay to talk out their situation. She turned her attention back to Anne. "Well, who do you think they were?"

"I spotted their vehicle down the road and walked by it, kind of casual like. I saw a small tag on the bumper that said U.S. Government, but the vehicle wasn't green like that of the Forest Service."

"Hmm...That's interesting," Kathleen said, wondering who the surveyors could be. "Thanks for calling me. I'll do some checking around."

Kathleen hung up the phone and walked over to the kitchen sink where she finished putting coffee in the coffee pot, which Richard had only begun. She sat down at the table to wait for the coffee to perk and covered her face with her hands, suddenly feeling the heaviness of their sin descend again upon her soul.

"God, what have I done?" It was a question she asked herself all too frequently.

CHAPTER 29

MEMO

To: Kathleen Sullivan
From: Jack Berens
Subject: Environmentalists

I know Sedona's filled with more than its share of crackpots, each spouting their own hyperbole, but this guy, John Perkins, takes the cake. I may be an avowed environmentalist, but Perkins is so rabid that he makes trouble on purpose at every city council or Forest Service meeting. See if this guy is for real.

John Perkins
"I Love This Land"
By Kathleen Sullivan
The *Sedona Chronicle*

For John Perkins, this land is everything.

He's not ashamed to say that loud and clear no matter what the community of Sedona might think about him and his radical pro-environmental viewpoint.

John Perkins is not afraid to fight for what he believes, and it's the land he believes in, not mankind and most certainly not the city of Sedona.

John is nearly 74 years old. A thin, wiry man who never takes off his half-glasses—looking at whomever he is speaking to over the top of them, giving him a constant quizzical look. He is considered an extremist by those who want the area to develop.

He came to Sedona about two years ago from the San Francisco area after his wife, Millie, died. He says he returned because the beauty of Sedona called to him through the years. John had worked as an extra on some of the movies that were filmed in Sedona in the 1940s and 1950s, movies like "Station West" with Dick Powell and "Broken Arrow" with James Stewart, and he never forgot the splendor of the place.

The old man likes to reminisce about those days, how wonderful they were.

"Oh, God! It was so beautiful here then. Sedona was barely a town, only a few places here then like the old Oak Creek Tavern, a gas station, a few motels, homes and ranches. It was wide open, and the sky was black as a cave at night with millions of twinkling lights. There were no neon lights like now to ruin the beauty of this place!" he remembers, banging his fist on his kitchen table for emphasis.

John lives in an old, cramped trailer at Rainbow Trailer Park in Oak Creek Canyon with his tabby cat, Pushy, who loves everybody that steps through the door, purring loudly in response to a scratch behind the ears. The avowed environmentalist says he lives in the canyon because it hasn't changed like Sedona. The smell of campfires still fill the evening air, the sound of Oak Creek can always be heard, and the canyon walls can never be touched by developers.

But John can't stand what has happened to change the town of Sedona since he first saw her rugged beauty those many years ago. When he returned two years ago, John says he was so upset at what he saw that he vowed to put a halt to Sedona's vicious growth.

"The buildings, the traffic! Why, it's even a city! What a disgrace to this precious country. These people move in here and want all the amenities of Los Angeles or Phoenix in this little town. Hell, it just can't be! So what if we have a few bumpy, dirt roads and everyone has a septic system?

"Now that damn city has come along and is putting in that even more damnable sewer system that's costing millions. And for what purpose? Because the yuppies and the rich retired people who move here want a perfect city, including a policeman and a fire station on every corner to protect their jewelry, furs, and art work."

He leans over the kitchen table and bangs his fist again. "You know what this place is? It's like a city of refugees. Everyone fleeing for their lives from modern America, wanting to come to some place rural to 'find' themselves, and when they get here, they bring all their anger, discontentment, and city ways with them. Why in the hell don't they stay away and leave this glorious place alone?"

Because of his feelings, John can be seen at every Forest Service meeting, every city council meeting, every Keep Sedona Beautiful meeting, every meeting where the Arizona Department of Transportation speaks about containing rock falls in Oak Creek Canyon or widening the two state highways that run through the area.

"There are those of us who don't want nothing done to this fine country anymore. Nothing! We're tired of the developers, the Realtors, the tourists, the city council. We don't want any more crappy tourist shops, ritzy restaurants, and yuppie homes with their guard gates. We want zero growth. Do you hear that, zero growth?"

For John Perkins, land exchanges are akin to Satan. His only hope to keep Sedona from growing larger is to hammer the Forest Service about its policy of exchanging land with developers. More land traded to developers only means more subdivisions, more buildings on land that should remain pristine, John says.

John's strategy is to keep his presence before the U.S. Forest Service on a repeated basis by visiting the Sedona District Ranger, the supervisor of the Coconino National Forest, and by firing off nasty letters to the Forest Service's southwest regional office in Albuquerque.

"I know the city fathers and the Forest Service bureaucrats get tired of seeing me at all these meetings, and they are probably sick of my letters. But I'll keep bugging them until I die! The bureaucrats want growth, growth, growth so they can get tax money into their money-grubbing hands. All the Forest Service wants to do is trade its land away to developers so they won't have to care for it any more. And all I want for them to do is stop!

"I don't think it's too much to ask these politicians and bureaucrats to just sit and think a minute before they approve this subdivision, this or that city improvement, or those damn land exchanges," John laments, jabbing his finger in the air to make his point.

John is particularly upset about the proposed Edgarville land exchange.

"By gum, I'll do anything and everything I can to stop that. Doesn't seem right that a hundred acres will be given up for ten. And then the Buckleys can just do what they damn well please out there. Money talks in Sedona, boy it sure does!"

His hand shakes a little as he sips his cup of strong, black coffee. He has a mound of papers, documents, and letters on his kitchen table, fighting the good fight, to keep the red earth of Sedona from being over built.

"I love this land. It's almost holy to me. I know there are those who laugh at this funny-looking old man who has his say at every meeting. I know there are those who think I'm nuts. But I'm not. I know what I know. And as sure as God is in His heaven, I know that this area will be ruined if we don't do something about it now. Others may talk about it, but I'm doing my best to stop it every day."

John looks out the small window of his trailer at the walls of Oak Creek Canyon and shakes his head.

"After all, once it's gone, it's gone. We can never get back to the beauty of just the red earth, the green forest, and the blue sky. Never!"

Chapter 30

The next morning, when Kathleen sat down at her desk, she found a small red pouch lying next to her computer.

A New Age prayer book beside the pouch explained the substance inside was copal, a resin that releases a sweet-scented smoke used in Native American blessing ceremonies. The smoke is believed to purify the environment and charge the atmosphere for prayer.

"Hi, Kathleen. I see you've found the copal I brought you," Lauren said, plopping herself down at her desk next to Kathleen. She reached down and tied the laces on her black granny boots.

"I did, Lauren. But, tell me, what's it for?"

Kathleen was puzzled by the gift. She picked up the small pouch and felt the smoothness of the red material, guessing it to be some sort of rayon or silk.

"The other day, when you came in and you looked so upset, I decided you needed spiritual guidance. We—those of us who call ourselves New Agers—have taken some of the traditions of Native Americans and incorporated them into our own ceremonies. I brought you this pouch of copal because it's supposed to give clarity and protection. Looking at you the other day, I would say you need some clarity in your life. You seem very confused. Personally, I think you're passing through dark energy."

Kathleen gave a short, unmirthful laugh. "Yes, I suppose you could say that. Thanks, Lauren. I appreciate your thoughtfulness."

"Well, I hope you use it. Just go out somewhere, away from everyone, and drop the copal on a few hot coals of charcoal. As the smoke rises, try to realign yourself with Spirit."

"Spirit?"

"Yes. Your inner guide, God, your guardian angel, anyone whom you feel protects you. Then pray, envisioning yourself surrounded by a protective circle. Remember always that the power of God protects you and the love of God enfolds you. Wherever you are, God is, and all is well. That's a prayer we often say."

Kathleen opened the red pouch and touched the copal. "How I wish I could believe that."

"You can make your own reality, Kathleen." There was a serious tone in Lauren's voice. She flicked her hand through her straight, black hair.

Kathleen looked over at her co-worker. "You really believe that, don't you?"

"Of course," Lauren said calmly, as if she were finishing a sermon. "Life would be better for you if you believed it too."

Kathleen did not answer. She wasn't sure what she believed. She felt buffeted by her Roman Catholic upbringing, Richard's powerful born-again Christian beliefs that she had succumbed to in a moment of emotional panic, and the persistent philosophies of the New Age. All I want right now is peace, she thought. With that in mind, she brushed aside her theological confusion and began to concentrate on the telephone conversation last night with Anne Brooks.

Why a federal agency other than the Forest Service would be surveying the Edgarville property, Kathleen wondered. Maybe Anne Brooks was wrong and it was the Forest Service. She picked up the telephone and dialed the Sedona District Ranger.

"Hi, Matt. This is Kathleen Sullivan with the *Chronicle*. You know I've been covering this story on the Buckley land exchange. Yesterday, a source mentioned to me that there were men out surveying the Edgarville property. Were they from your office?"

Matt Reynolds said he was unaware of a Forest Service survey crew working near Edgarville. He suggested she call the Coconino National Forest headquarters in Flagstaff. "The big guns are working on this one, Kathleen. Not us peons in Sedona."

That terse, off-the-cuff comment raised the ante for Kathleen. Now she really wanted to know what was going on. She dialed headquarters and was transferred to several different people who also had no information. In frustration, Kathleen finally asked for the public information officer, Caroline Tiffin.

Caroline's perky voice came over the line. "Hi, Kathleen. What can I do for you?"

Kathleen asked who would be dealing with the Buckley land exchange at headquarters.

"Oh, that's Aaron Stein. He's not in his office today, but I can leave a message to have him call you."

Kathleen decided to lie. "Well, I'm on a tight deadline. Is there anyone else there that knows how it's coming along?"

"I was in a staff meeting this week and heard a little about it. I'm not sure if what I know will help you, however."

"Anything will help," Kathleen said, pressing her.

"Aaron said he received an urgent memo from the southwest regional office in Albuquerque stating the need to complete the exchange as fast as possible because some other federal agency is negotiating with the Buckley Corporation for that land. Ordinarily, a land exchange can take up to 18 months or longer because we have an environmental process to go though. But Aaron said if the property is needed by the U.S. Government for military or security reasons it can be processed quickly through the law of eminent domain."

The public information officer's statement seemed to corroborate what Anne Brooks told Kathleen.

"Any idea what federal agency is in such a rush for that property?" Kathleen asked.

"No. Aaron didn't say. All I know is that the forest supervisor asked Aaron for a copy of the memo from Albuquerque."

"How can I get a copy of that memo, Caroline?"

The public information officer suddenly sounded hesitant as if she realized she may have said too much to Kathleen. "Uh...I'm not sure, Kathleen. No one in upper management is around for me to ask. They're all attending a seminar in Phoenix. Can I have Aaron give you a call when he comes in?"

Kathleen knew Caroline was beginning to backtrack. "Sure. Please have him call me as soon as he comes in tomorrow."

"Well, I'm not sure if he'll be in tomorrow. But I'll try." The perkiness was gone from her voice.

"Thanks for your help, Caroline," Kathleen said, trying to seem less interested in the memo than she was.

Kathleen's next call was to Albuquerque. There the public information officer for the southwest regional office told Kathleen in a terse tone that the memo sent to Aaron Stein was not a public document that it was marked confidential, and therefore it did not have to be released to the press.

"I should think you would know that confidential interagency memos are not covered by the Freedom of Information Act." There was a note of triumph in the public information officer's voice.

Kathleen cursed under her breath when she heard the memo was confidential and flung the telephone into its receiver with a bang.

"Yes, goddamn it, I know about confidential memos. I was just hoping you didn't."

Kathleen mentally sifted through her sources, wondering who would be able to find out for her why another federal agency was surveying the Edgarville property.

A thought came to her about Jeremy Slater, the aide to Davis Meade, Arizona's U.S. Senator. She knew Slater when she worked for the *Los Angeles Times*. During that period, Slater was the aide to a California senator who left the U.S. Senate to run for governor. When he lost, Slater went to work for Meade.

She lifted the receiver and dialed his number. "Hi, Jeremy, this is Kathleen Sullivan."

"Well, if it isn't the wandering reporter! Last I heard you left the *Arizona Republic* to work for a small newspaper in Sedona. Life must be good in beautiful Sedona." His voice sounded lighthearted.

"Yeah, well. Sedona isn't..."

Jeremy chuckled, interrupting her. "Come on Kathleen! The state Office of Tourism wouldn't like your attitude."

When she did not respond, his tone changed because he realized she was serious. "What's cooking?"

"Plenty. I'm hung up on a story here about a land trade." She explained the circumstances to him and took a deep breath, her voice trembling a bit. "Jeremy, I need a favor. I've done a few for you through the years, and I've never asked for anything in return."

"Yes, Kathleen. I know that. What do you want?" His answer was cautious.

"I just want to know what federal agency is in negotiation for that land with the Buckleys. I want to know why there's such a rush to exchange the land. Wouldn't this have to go through some kind of a public hearing, some court approval first?"

"I'm not sure, Kathleen. You and I both know lots of things are done by the government without public hearings or court approval. In my book, it's called high-handed federal edict. I'll do some nosing around and see what can find. By the way, isn't there some conflict of interest for you with this story, being a Buckley and all?"

"There would have been if I were a beneficiary of my husband's will, which I'm not. But to be honest, there still is a conflict of interest I suppose because I'm connected by marriage to the Buckleys. But I've been tipped about this government survey, and I'm naturally curious about what my dear husband's family is up to." Her voice was sarcastic.

"Besides, this could really be a big story if the government is trying to sneak something on that property like a nuclear waste dump. I feel the public's need to know is greater than my conflict of interest."

Jeremy laughed. "You know, Kathleen, not everything the government does is some sort of a conspiracy. Mostly, it's expediency."

But she was serious. "Maybe so, Jeremy. But anything involving the Buckleys is suspect, in my opinion. I realize, of course, that I'm highly prejudiced."

"I understand, Kathleen. Well, you might also want to check with the federal court. Maybe some papers have been filed with Judge Oswald."

Kathleen was silent for a moment as she tried to grasp what Jeremy said. "Judge Oswald? You don't mean Judge Kenneth Oswald, do you? He's the superior court judge who presided over Scott's will."

"Well, he's not a superior court judge anymore. He got bumped up to the federal bench in early November by the President. Judge Martha Kirby retired the end of October, and the vacancy needed to be filled quickly because of the court's heavy load, although I must admit the appointment and quick confirmation by the Senate sure came as a surprise. In my opinion, Oswald doesn't have that much experience to be a federal judge."

Kathleen was silent for a long time.

"Hey, Kathleen? Are you still there?"

"Yeah, Jeremy. I'm sorry. That news caught me off guard for a minute." She tried to control the shakiness in her voice. "Look, I really appreciate your looking into this for me. Please find out all you can. You know that no one will ever know you're my source."

"Yes, I know. You're a damn good reporter, Kathleen. Maybe you should go back to the *Times*. That paper would better appreciate your talents."

"I'll give that a thought," she said as she hung up the telephone.

She had felt queasy all morning, but this unsettling news about Judge Oswald forced her to run to the bathroom.

Maybe—she thought as she washed her face in the sink trying to get rid of the smell of vomit—just maybe her queasiness was because she smelled a rat, a thoroughly rotten rat.

CHAPTER 31

Discouraged that she was not able to find any information quickly about the surveyors and suspicious about Judge Oswald's sudden appointment to the federal bench, Kathleen tried later that afternoon to talk to Jack about the story and its implications.

To her surprise, Jack was impatient with her.

"Look, Kathleen. I don't think this is much of a story. So what if the feds are out surveying the property? Some environmental do-gooder calls you and thinks the land is going to be raped by the government and you get all hot under the collar. You don't have any kind of proof."

"I would if I could get hold of that confidential memo," she answered.

"I said I don't think there's a story." There was a nasty edge to his voice.

Kathleen could feel her Irish temper rising.

"You didn't feel that way when you originally wanted me to do the story on the people who live in Edgarville, those who are upset about the land trade. What if the government is planning to put something on that land that would be worse than a goddamn housing development? Those people are already mad at the government, God only knows what their reaction to something else would be. I don't understand you! Now when I have the possibility of proof that something underhanded is going on, you're suddenly not interested. What gives?"

Jack simply shrugged his shoulders, but Kathleen did not give up. "Look, Jack, it's the paper trail I'm looking for, and I thought you might have some ideas. If I had the proof, this newspaper would have one hell of a story, the kind that would bring the *Chronicle* the hard-hitting reputation you want. But I need some help! Editors and reporters normally discuss stories and how to approach them, where to look for information. You've done none of that as long as I've been here except hand me one of your goddamn memos!" Her voice shook.

Jack's face turned red with anger.

"That may be the case with some guy getting $50,000 a year who does nothing but edit. But those guys aren't also running the financial end of a newspaper. I am. I don't have time to sit and discuss stories with you, Kathleen. You're basically on your own. This newspaper is, as you've probably guessed, in financial trouble. I could discuss stories with you all day and that wouldn't bring in the money that pays your salary. Again, my feeling is that there is no story and you should just drop it."

Losing her temper, she burst out, "God, what a hard-headed bastard you are!"

He ignored her comment and continued to press his point.

"As for Philip Buckley and Judge Oswald, you don't have any proof there either. You couldn't prove that Oswald threw you off the will and then Buckley paid him off through his influence with the White House. That's pretty far-fetched, Kathleen. Frankly, I think you're a little too sensitive about Philip Buckley. He isn't the monster you make him out to be. He's a pretty big man in this state. In fact, I've heard the governor is going to name him Arizona Man of the Year because of the incredible growth of the various Buckley enterprises."

"Really?" Kathleen asked, bitterly mulling over that news for a moment. "I wasn't aware that you knew Philip."

"I don't know him, but I've seen him socially." Jack did not look at her as he dropped that bit of news.

"Socially? Socially, meaning what?" Kathleen suddenly felt fear gnaw at her innards.

"We had lunch the other day. It was just a business lunch. Philip is simply attempting to keep in touch with the community since his brother's death."

Jack's anger subsided and he tried to placate her with a pleasant tone, but she would have none of it.

"Yeah, I'll bet. Did he by chance ask you to keep me off the land trade story?"

"Don't be silly, Kathleen. He just wanted to meet with me, considering I own the second largest newspaper in the area."

Kathleen stood staring at Jack for a moment, saying nothing. She walked back to her desk and in a fit of anger picked up the red copal pouch Lauren gave her and shoved it and the New Age prayer book into her handbag.

"I've got some contacts to see," she said in a low tone as she walked toward the front door, then slammed it shut as she stepped out onto the sidewalk filled with tourists.

Later, after Lauren also left the office for the day, Jack picked up the phone and dialed a Phoenix number. After a moment, the deep voice of Philip Buckley came on the line.

"Good afternoon, Philip, this is Jack Berens. I've been thinking very carefully about your offer and I've decided to accept it."

Jack was silent for a few moments, listening to the other man speak.

"I think we can close the deal in two weeks...Let's see, today is the tenth. That would mean the last issue of the paper would be Christmas Eve Day. Yes, that would be fine. Call me when the papers are drawn up. Again, I want you to know I appreciate your generous offer."

He felt the stress of financial worries drain from his body and he laughed to himself. Well, Kathleen, he thought, you don't have much time to get your Pulitzer Prize winning story into print.

CHAPTER 32

For years, whenever Kathleen was troubled because of her relationship with Scott, she would drive to the Chapel of the Holy Cross, the small, austere Roman Catholic chapel rising in the lee of Twin Buttes, about three miles south of midtown Sedona.

The chapel boasts a 90-foot-high cross which bisects the face of the structure and commands an expansive view of Courthouse Butte and Bell Rock. The inverted wedge of concrete, aggregate, and glass always offered Kathleen much more than a view.

The sculptress who commissioned the chapel in 1953 called it a spiritual fortress so charged with God that it spurred man's spirit Godward. Kathleen felt that to be true from the moment she first set eyes on the chapel. For her, this church was truly God's shelter among the red rocks, not some prayer wheel on a deserted mesa. This was His place. This was where she came to be near Him when her soul was as troubled as it was now.

As she walked up the steep ramp to the church courtyard, the scenery enveloped her soul. Large billowy white clouds played tag with the sun, causing shadows to rise and fall over the red rock formations.

Although the courtyard was filled with its usual mob of tourists taking photographs, there were few people inside the chapel itself. She made the sign of the cross and genuflected quickly before the altar, then Kathleen sat down in the front pew, near the row of lighted candles.

She sat for a long time, listening to the sounds of the church: the lyrical Gregorian chants that echoed over the speaker system, the squeaking of wood as people kneeled to pray, the whispers of prayers, and the smell of candles burning in supplication for unanswered desires.

And then she began praying, asking for guidance, something she had not done for a long time. Kathleen felt uneasy praying while she sat, so she kneeled on the hard floor between the altar and the front pew, wanting to feel closer to God.

As she prayed, a cloud bartering with the sun caused a shaft of light to fall momentarily on Kathleen through the huge window behind the altar.

She looked up into the light, and saw the bronze sculpted face of Jesus Christ that hangs at the apex of the huge cross bisecting the front of the church. The sculpture was outlined by the sun, causing her to gasp. The light made the sculpture look like a holy apparition and she was filled with the wonder of it.

Thoughts of her life with Scott flowed into her mind like the sun flowed in through the window, and she realized her separation from God and the Roman Catholic Church came because of the desolation she felt as her marriage crumbled. Rather than looking closely at herself, she chose to blame everyone else—Father O'Malley, the church and, finally, God for all that happened to her—when she was the one who needed to take responsibility for her miserable life with Scott.

Her knees began to ache and her lower back cried out for relief, but Kathleen did not move from her kneeling position as she tried to fathom the meaning of her relationship with Richard.

Painful as it was, Kathleen pushed her mind to review the past months and she began to perceive that the sins she committed with Richard were no different than her relationship with Scott. In both cases, she let herself become a victim for the want of both men's love.

It was the same with her taking on the mantle of a born-again Christian. She made her proclamation for Richard's sake, wanting him to love her more, not because she wanted to save her own soul.

She was, now more than ever, a lost Catholic, searching for God and herself amid the rubble of her life. The beauty of the Roman Catholic traditions and sacraments were so much a part of her she realized that she could never give them up for any other religious philosophy.

Still praying for the guidance she so desperately needed, she stood up and lit a candle, watching the smoke of the flame move up the wall. Kathleen knew her prayer was no different than the thousands of others before her who lit candles and prayed to God seeking answers to their petitions.

So many, in fact, that the wall was black from their flames.

When Kathleen arrived home, she found Richard sitting in her front room, reading the Bible he gave her for her birthday. He looked up at her as she sat her purse on the kitchen counter. It was a strange look—one she never saw before, unnerving her. She didn't understand his expression until he walked into the kitchen and pointed to a passage in Proverbs.

> "Trust in the Lord with all your heart,
> And lean not on your own understanding;
> In all your ways acknowledge Him,
> And He shall direct your paths."

"This is what I must do, Kathleen." Richard's voice was hard even as he gently placed the Bible on the kitchen counter.

She looked at him, wondering what he would say next, trying to prepare herself for it. He seemed angry, but more than that, he seemed separated from her in some final way.

"I love God more than either of you," he said referring to Kathleen and his wife. "I can no longer go against His Commandments."

She touched his arm, but he moved it from her and she was instantly angered by his reaction. She knew by his lovemaking the past few days, after they had resumed their affair that it was lust that drove him to her, not the love she felt for him. Yet, she felt the need to explain her love for him in the hope he would understand her.

"I love you, Richard, more than I have ever loved anyone. Because of that love, because of my wanting you, because of my fear of losing you, I would do anything for you, including losing my own sense of self, my own soul. Yes, my own soul! But you have made it apparent that you no longer want me. I'm just a piece of flesh your body needs until you become so sodden with guilt, like now, that you turn back to God in your sinful anguish. I'm sick of it! Sick of your wanting me and then crying to God because of your guilt. You're like a child!"

He was silent, acting almost as if he did not hear her. She reached in her purse to drop the keys she still held in her hand, and took out the small copal pouch, placing it on the counter next to the Bible. She began making coffee, needing it to strengthen her nerves.

Richard saw the pouch and grabbed it. "What's this?" he nearly shouted, dangling the pouch from its string.

"What?" She looked up from her chore, surprised by the tone of his voice.

"It's something the New Agers use in their meditations. Lauren gave it to me."

He opened it up, smelled it and walked over to the sink, dumping the resin, washing it away.

"That's devil worship! That's New Age bullshit! What the hell are you doing with that, you who have asked Jesus to be your savior? Are you recanting that vow?" he shouted.

Kathleen reacted in fury. "You don't have any right to throw away something that was given to me in the spirit of friendship even if it is New Age! I don't happen to believe your drivel about devil worship. That's the problem with you born-again Christians, you think Satan's lurking behind anything and everything that doesn't conform to your own beliefs."

Richard lurched at her, grabbing her by the shoulders, shaking her, fury in his eyes.

"Are you mocking God? You are, I know you are! How dare you...you whore!"

He raised his right hand as if to slap her but she stood fast, looking him straight in the face. Just as suddenly, he dropped both of his hands and stepped back, his eyes wide from the terror of his action, his words.

"Well, Richard, I wonder what kind of hell there is for those of us who pretend to be Christians, but really are no better than the Pharisees."

He stood, mute and then buried his face in his hands. When he looked at her, his eyes were full of tears. "This is a sin I can no longer live with," his voice was soft, sad.

She picked up the Bible he gave her and handed it back to him. "That's the difference between us, Richard. For me, God is revealed in the love between a man and a woman. I always felt in the love we had for one another, we were worshiping God. You only saw it as a sin."

She turned her back on him and moved to the kitchen sink, where she looked out the window at the view of Coffee Pot Rock.

After a moment, she turned back to him and said in a quiet, controlled tone, "The rest of your life you will hunger for this love that you have wanted all of your life, and you will question yourself and God as to why you gave it up.

"And the rest of my life I will question God because you did give it up, and I will be tortured by it."

CHAPTER 33

The days came and went, but there was no solace for Kathleen's heartache.

She stumbled through the interminable hours like a drunkard, craving even a word from Richard, knowing there would be none, hoping nevertheless. Her withdrawal from him was so painful at times she could barely get through each day, let alone her work at the newspaper.

Even the weather matched her mood. It was gray and rainy. December usually brought cold, crisp weather to northern Arizona, but never this much rain.

As Christmas drew nearer, Kathleen noticed Jack seemed less worried about the affairs of his business. In a jovial mood one day, he told Kathleen and Lauren that the newspaper office would be closed between Dec. 24 and New Year's Day.

"It's a little treat to both of you for working so hard. You'll have the time off and get paid for it."

Lauren looked incredulous. "If the paper's closed, I guess that means we're not putting out an issue for New Year's. What about the restaurants and hotels who want to advertise about New Year's Eve festivities?"

Jack's answer was quick. "That's an easy problem to solve, Lauren. You can notify your advertisers for the Christmas issue that there will be no issue for New Year's. If the hotels and restaurants want to advertise about New Year's, they can do it then."

Lauren shrugged her shoulders in disgust. When Jack left for lunch, Lauren said to Kathleen, "Something doesn't smell right. Why would he close the newspaper for more than a week? That doesn't make sense."

"Nothing he does makes sense," Kathleen responded.

Along with her other writing assignments, Kathleen continued to work on the land trade story whenever Jack was out of the office, calling various people in the community who might know what was happening.

She probed her sources connected with Keep Sedona Beautiful, the Audubon Society, and Anne Brooks. Anne reiterated her suspicions, but no one else had seen or heard anything unusual. She even called John Perkins, the environmentalist she profiled several weeks before.

John listened intently to Kathleen's explanation about a survey party and the confidential Forest Service memo.

"Well, Kathleen, my personal opinion is that despite those in the Forest Service who are intent on land trades, there are a few who disagree with that policy. They keep their mouths shut, but I know who they are. I'll check around and see if I can get anything for you."

She thanked him and added, "You've given me some hope, John."

He chuckled. "Anything for a pretty lady. Say, by the way, Kathleen, I should have told you this before, but that article you did about me...well, it correctly showed my feelings about this land. I thank you for that. Most reporters make fun of me. You didn't."

"That's nice to hear, John," Kathleen said. "In this business, we usually hear when someone dislikes a story we've done. We hardly ever receive a compliment. Take Norma Hopkins, for instance, you know the actress who lives here and in New York. She was furious about the article I did on her saying I portrayed her as a rich bitch." There was a hint of mirth in Kathleen's voice.

"She is kid, she is. But I bet she didn't tell you that she never made it in the movies. I know because we worked together on a movie shot here in Sedona years ago, and she never got another offer by a studio. That's why she stayed in New York, working on the stage. I guess they put up with that kind of behavior in the theater. Anyway, Kathleen, I'll snoop around for that memo. You'll hear from me."

On December 23, Kathleen was alone in the office, thumbing through her notes on the land trade, trying to put together pieces of the puzzle. She had no place special to go, so she busied herself with cleaning her desk before the office closed for the holidays.

Suddenly, the front door opened, and she realized the man walking through it was Jeremy Slater, the aide to U.S. Senator Davis Meade.

Kathleen always thought Jeremy was a handsome man, with thick blond hair and a nicely trimmed mustache. He was tall and thin, and he looked as impeccable as ever. Jeremy Slater was well respected in the political community. He had a quiet way about him that made people trust him, and Kathleen was one of those people.

"Jeremy! My God, what a surprise!" she exclaimed, shaking his hand. "What brings you up this way?"

"Oh, I've got an important meeting to attend in Flagstaff on that proposed Navajo-Hopi land trade, and I thought I could catch you for a cup of coffee."

"Oh, that would be wonderful! Just what I need on such a dreary, rainy day. How about that little coffee shop down by the highway intersection, the Ranch Kitchen?"

As they slogged through the downpour and got into Jeremy's sedan, Kathleen looked closer at him. About 10 years younger than herself, he looked worn. His blond hair was beginning to creep back a little from his crown and his eyes had more crinkles around them than she remembered.

"How are you, anyway! It's been a long time since I've seen you. Tell me, do you like working for Meade?"

Jeremy nodded, but there was a weary tone in his voice. "Oh, he keeps me hopping. There's no down time in Meade's office. I have to say he works hard for his constituents."

A few minutes later they were sitting in a corner of the small coffee shop, away from some wet tourists who wandered in off the street.

They sat quietly while the server, a young Mexican man with a large gold cross around his neck, poured the steaming coffee.

"What's up, Jeremy? I have a feeling you have something to tell me."

"You're right, Kathleen. I do have some information. It comes from a source who I personally know is very reliable. But he absolutely cannot be quoted on the record, nor will he be a source for background information."

Kathleen gave him a look of disdain. "What the hell does that mean?"

"It means I know what's happening with that Edgarville property but you have no way to prove it," he answered bluntly.

Kathleen sat quietly for a few moments, thinking about Jeremy's remark. "How did you find out the information?"

"By sheer coincidence—luck, whatever you want to call it. I have a... friend in Washington who works for the Justice Department. We were discussing Judge Oswald's appointment to the federal bench, and I happened to mention your telephone call to me about the land trade. It was then that he told me his boss has met with Philip Buckley on several occasions."

He took a deep breath, the kind one makes before entering the confessional, and leaned forward toward Kathleen.

"In fact," Jeremy said, his eyes lowered, "this friend was my former lover when I lived in Washington before I moved to Arizona to work for Senator Meade. My friend has a high-level position in the Justice Department, and the leak could easily be traced back to him and then to me because of our former relationship. This is very sensitive, Kathleen—both the information about the land trade and our sexual preferences."

"Can you at least tell me what is happening with the property?"

"Sure, but it will do you no good because at this stage there are only verbal negotiations going on between the top guns at Justice and Philip Buckley. There's no paper trail from that end. You could probe all you want, but everything would be denied."

She looked him straight in the eye. "Look, Jeremy, I've always suspected you were gay. I'm not shocked by your revelation. You've been honest and up front with me, and I appreciate that now. I understand that your source of information is in a vulnerable position, as are you."

"Yes. We are. Our life's work is at stake. No matter what the gay rights groups say, coming out of the closet is disastrous for one's career, particularly in the federal government."

She nodded her head, understanding his predicament, but pressed him for more information. "Look, I'm simply interested in finding out who Philip Buckley is dealing with. It's up to me to find the proof for your tip."

Jeremy took a deep gulp of coffee and looked around the coffee shop. He lowered his voice enough that Kathleen had to lean over the table to hear him.

"It's the Attorney General."

Her dark eyebrows raised. She also looked around the coffee shop to see if anyone was listening.

"You're joking! What does the Attorney General have to do with a hundred acres of mesquite brush near Sedona?"

He took a gulp of air, as if he were drowning. "I…guess you need to know the whole story. It's incredible…but if this deal goes through, the site will house a small maximum security federal prison. But it's who the feds plan to keep there that's the real kicker."

Kathleen's eyes narrowed, trying to discern what he was talking about. "What do you mean who? Isn't it bad enough the government wants to put a prison on that site? Those people out in Edgarville will have a goddamn fit, and I wouldn't blame them." There was a note of anger in her voice.

Jeremy looked down at his cup of coffee, and hesitated to answer.

"Well? Tell me the rest!" she urged. "I've got to know the rest! Please!"

His voice was even lower. "Look, Kathleen, this is going to sound far-fetched. I know you won't believe it, but it's true. It's incredible, but true. My friend has been in on the discussions."

He took a sip of coffee and she noticed his hand was shaking.

She laughed suddenly. "I'm sorry, Jeremy. This sounds so cloak and dagger!"

"Oh, I know," she said suddenly in a mocking tone, an idea popping into her head. "It's a place to imprison those militia types. You know, those who are madder than hell about the siege at Waco, and the deaths of the Branch Davidians."

He looked up from his coffee, straight into Kathleen's eyes. "That's right, Kathleen."

Her response was to laugh at him, loud enough so that the people on the other side of the room looked over at her.

"Jesus Christ! You sound as paranoid as those idiots out in Edgarville. Those people haven't done anything but talk about revolution. We have a right to talk about whatever we want in this country, including revolution. Still...I can't believe a revolution would ever happen in America or that we would need a prison to house these who march around in their camouflage gear!"

His voice was tired. "Kathleen...The FBI has information that those people who are angry at what happened in Texas are forming armed militias. These groups believe their constitutional rights are going to be taken away because Congress is considering stiffer gun laws. They're saying they love their country but hate their government, and the only way to change it will be through revolution, a bloody revolution." Fear was in his voice.

He continued. "Those in the know at Justice are beginning to hear rumblings that these people are planning something terrible for what happened at Waco."

"Oh, for Christ's sake, Jeremy! I can't believe Americans would do something like that. Frankly I think paranoia reigns at Justice. Is there some concrete evidence these militia types will perpetrate some act of revenge?"

"Yes. One scenario we are hearing from sources who have infiltrated these militia groups is the bombing of a federal building filled with federal employees...ordinary people like me just doing their job. Another is the murder of members of the Supreme Court while they are sitting in session. We just don't know where or when these violent acts might happen."

Kathleen was silent. "But why build such a prison here, near Sedona? Why not hidden in the wilds of Montana or North Dakota?"

"Because Arizona is a red neck state. There's lots of those militia groups forming in Arizona, according to the FBI. Sedona is a great place to make a public statement, you know...something as malignant as a federal maximum security prison housing violent militiamen near these beautiful, spiritual red rocks."

Then he said softly, as if musing philosophically, "The government is supposed to be the protector of the land, sort of like a husband is to his wife. Putting a prison for radicals in this beautiful place is as horrible as a wife raped by her own husband."

Kathleen felt a jolt go through her body. She kept her eyes down, so he couldn't see her horror. She sipped her cold coffee, holding onto the cup with both hands so Jeremy couldn't see them tremble. The information began to seep into her.

"Well, the puzzle fits. Judge Oswald throwing me off Scott's will so I couldn't interfere with the land trade. Judge Oswald handily picked through Philip's influence to be a federal judge in the district where a hundred acres owned by the Buckley family is going to be taken by the feds through eminent domain, no doubt appraised at the highest value. God, it was all done so neat and tidy!"

Jeremy shook his head. "It's not done yet, Kathleen."

She looked at him. "Do you realize how big this story is?"

"Yes, I do."

She was angry now. "Goddamn it, Jeremy! I've got to prove what's going on before I can write a story! I can't just write it on hearsay."

"I told you, everything is verbal at this stage. That memo between offices of the Forest Service is the only concrete piece of evidence that spells out who is negotiating with Philip Buckley. Some memo-happy bureaucrat left a paper trail. That's your only hope."

CHAPTER 34

Christmas Eve Day dawned with a northern Arizona storm warning. An unusual storm of warm, heavy rain was slowly moving up the state from the Gulf of Mexico. Weather forecasters were predicting snow melt from the peaks above Flagstaff.

The rain from previous days already swelled Oak Creek as it washed down the canyon, causing police officials to keep an eye on the rising water level under the bridge at Tlaquepaque. With the new storm warning, communities along the creek, particularly in Oak Creek Canyon, were being warned about possible flooding.

Kathleen woke that day with a sense of haste.

Her conversation with Jeremy Slater weighed on her mind all night. She wasn't sure she believed it, despite what Jeremy said. Yet the information was disturbing enough that her intuition as a reporter told her she couldn't discount it, particularly with Philip Buckley and Judge Oswald somehow involved.

If she could prove such negotiations were going on between the U.S. Attorney General and Philip Buckley, and get the story in print, maybe there would be enough of a public outcry to squelch the deal. It would be a particular plum for the *Chronicle* to publish the story with Philip Buckley about to be named Arizona Man of the Year by the governor. Surely Jack would see through his prejudices to break one of the biggest stories to hit the state. In fact, the story also had national implications.

She needed to talk again with John Perkins and tell him what she knew. Armed with that information, perhaps he could persuade one of his Forest Service friends to get a copy of the memo.

But first, before doing anything, Kathleen needed to confirm her suspicions about herself. She had gone to her gynecologist two days ago, and after discussing her various physical symptoms, Dr. Brown told her that despite her age, she could very well be pregnant. The onset of menopause did not preclude such a possibility, he said sadly, eyeing her over his half glasses.

He took a urine test, the results of which would be ready this morning.

She sat up in bed, contemplating the mess she found herself in, thinking ruefully that this was some Christmas present she had given herself: 46-years-old, unmarried, quite possibly pregnant by a married man who would never divorce his wife, who loved God more than he loved her. How could she bring a child into such a situation?

She shook her head to negate that thought, got up, put on her robe and thumbed through the telephone directory. Perkins was not listed, but she remembered she had his number in one of her notebooks at the office.

She grabbed a piece of toast, threw on her jeans and sweat shirt and headed for Uptown. Because of the early morning hour and the heavy rain, Kathleen found parking directly in front of the newspaper, a rare occurrence.

Just as Kathleen was about to put her key into the lock, she realized the door was slightly open. She pushed it and found herself looking into an empty room. The desks and computers were gone, old newspapers were flung on the floor in a pile. The back room where Jack Berens lived was empty except for a dirty mattress sitting forlornly on the floor with hangers thrown on top.

She stepped inside, slamming the door behind her.

"Goddamn it! I should have listened to myself when Jack told me he had lunch with Philip! I knew something was up, I just could feel it!" she cried aloud to the empty room. She realized Jack must have moved out last night after she left with Jeremy.

She stood for a moment in the middle of the bare room and suddenly felt the ground spin under her feet. A few moments later, when she came to, the room seemed out of focus, and she was shaking violently. Kathleen felt as if the ironclad jaws of deceit were closing in on her and she began to weep, softly at first, then with great surging sobs of pain and anger welling up from deep within her soul.

"The bastards! All of them, bastards!" she cried.

She sat in the dark, cold room, not moving for a long time when she heard the front door open. It was John Perkins.

"Kathleen! Is that you there?" The old man peered into the dark room, saw her slumped in the middle of the floor and rushed to help her up. She wiped her wet face with her hands, trying to gather herself.

"I was just sitting here crying my heart out," she answered in a small voice.

He patted her on the back, and looked about the empty room. "There, there girl. Things aren't so bad after all, although I reckon you don't have a newspaper any more to publish your articles in."

"You guessed right," she said with meaningful sarcasm.

"That's OK." John said. "That story you've been working on, the land trade—well I'm getting the information for you. Some big newspaper will take it, maybe the *Washington Post*."

"Are you serious, John?"

"Yes, ma'am. I talked to my friend yesterday who works at the Coconino National Forest headquarters. He was in that meeting where the memo was mentioned and said he was upset to hear the Buckley land exchange was being rushed through for national security reasons. He did some poking around late yesterday afternoon after I talked to him. The office closed early for a Christmas party at some restaurant in Flagstaff and he stayed behind, saying he had paperwork to clear up."

John Perkins smiled at Kathleen.

"Well, he's got a copy of the memo from Albuquerque. I know that's not exactly kosher, but get this! The Justice Department wants the land for a federal prison, pronto! I don't know why they need the land so fast, but pressure is coming down from the Attorney General to the head of the Forest Service."

John had a sparkle in his eye. He was proud of himself. "Look, I'm going up to Flagstaff to get the copy. I just stopped by to tell you because the operator said this phone was disconnected."

He looked around. "I guess she was right."

Kathleen felt a wave of relief. She gave him a long hug and he smiled.

"Why don't you come over to my little trailer this evening about six, and me and my cat, Pushy, we'll have a Christmas Eve supper ready for you. It won't be much, mind you,'cause I'm not much of a cook since my dear wife died. But my Christmas gift to you will be the memo."

Kathleen could barely believe what she heard.

"Oh, John! That would be wonderful! That would be simply wonderful!"

CHAPTER 35

Late that afternoon, Kathleen drove into the parking lot of St. John Vianney Catholic Church.

She turned off the engine and sat in the car watching the heavy rain fall on her windshield, listening to the relentless pounding of it on the roof. When would it stop, she wondered. It seemed ominous.

Off to the side of the church's parking lot she noticed the three large crosses, symbolic of that Good Friday so many centuries ago when Jesus Christ suffered the inequity of mankind's sins and the earth trembled and darkness fell. The crosses stood silent, impassive, like the red rocks shrouded in clouds. She shivered. The last time she was here was in April, at Scott's funeral.

She was afraid to go into the church where she cursed her husband's soul and damned her own soul because of her hatred. To Kathleen, even her adulterous love affair with Richard was not as sinful as that sacrilege.

The Bible that Richard gave her lay on the car seat beside her. Although she handed it back to him during their last horrible argument, he left it on the back porch before he drove away. Now she picked the holy book up, felt the smoothness of the leather, and tried to find the strength to face Father Timothy O'Malley.

She turned to Psalm 27, her favorite. The words seemed to apply to her fears of everyday life.

"The Lord is my light and my salvation;
Whom shall I fear?
The Lord is the strength of my life;
Of whom shall I be afraid?
When the wicked came against me
To eat up my flesh,
My enemies and foes,
They stumbled and fell..."

Her thoughts moved back to John Perkins and his good news about the memo. After she left the newspaper office, she went home and called her former editor at the *Arizona Republic*, explaining the entire story.

Lin Ellis was silent for a moment, then said, "It may take you a couple of days to get responses from Justice and the head of the Forest Service, Kathleen, but I see this as a story we can break on New Year's Day when the governor announces his Arizona Man of the Year Award. What a coup!"

Maybe, just maybe, Kathleen thought, this was the beginning of a new life. The story about the land trade was her chance to resurrect herself as a journalist. It was her way back, a way to climb out of the blackness she herself created by returning to Sedona and working for Jack Berens.

That was the secular way to save herself. But she knew the only way to save her soul was to face God and His servant, Father O'Malley, in the confessional.

Particularly now that she knew she carried Richard's child, Kathleen had to cleanse her soul if she was to bring this baby into the world, whole and bright and loved.

She took a deep breath and quickly opened the car door, making a dash for the church in the pouring rain. Inside, she found Father O'Malley making last minute preparations for the Christmas Eve Mass. He looked up when he heard the noise of the door into the church close behind her, and saw her standing there, dripping wet.

"Kathleen! My child!" the priest said, happiness in his voice.

She ran down the isle of the church toward him, and when she reached him, she buried her face in his black robe. He let her cry, patting her gently, overjoyed to see her return to grace.

They sat down in the front pew and spoke in quiet tones to one another. They did not need the formality of the confessional for Kathleen to seek forgiveness for her sins and for the priest to give her absolution. Her voice shook as she whispered to her priest, but the feeling of peace that eluded her for so long began to seep into her soul.

Kathleen bowed her head when she finished and the priest extended his hands over her and prayed, "God the Father of mercies..."

Before he let her perform her penance, the priest lightly touched her shoulder, wanting to reconcile her with God. His voice was gentle. "Kathleen... Perhaps you have not loved wisely.

But you have loved, as Jesus so loved us that He gave His life for our sins. Now...particularly, I think you understand that kind of love is worth losing everything for."

She lifted her head from her hands clasped together in supplication. A light shone in her eyes that had not been there for many years.

"Yes, Father," she answered, understanding at last. "It is."

Kathleen impatiently poked at the defrost button as she maneuvered her car out of the church parking lot. Although the windshield wipers were doing their job against the rain's onslaught, she couldn't see clearly because of the vapor that formed on the inside of the windshield. The defrost mechanism seemed to have suddenly quit.

She stopped for a moment at Soldiers Pass Road and pulled a handkerchief from her purse, wiping her side of the windshield, clearing it a little. The window stayed clear for only a short while, and Kathleen continued to fumble with the heater as she headed north on Highway 89A toward Oak Creek Canyon.

She thought about stopping to call John Perkins but remembered she never got his phone number. He would be waiting impatiently this Christmas Eve, anxious to gift her with the memo, she knew, and she was just as excited to receive the evidence she needed against Philip.

Suddenly, Kathleen felt alive again. Her return to grace through her confession lifted the hatred for Scott from her soul, and the oppression she felt because of her love affair with Richard was gone. All she needed now was that memo. The heater began to pull the fog off the sides of the windshield, and in an effort to see better, she rolled down the car window on her side, driving slowly, straining to see the white line in the center of the highway. Although she was getting wet, between the heater, her wiping the windshield and the open window, she made her way slowly up the canyon, her anxiety building as she thought about the furor her story would cause in the lofty political camps of Arizona and Washington.

Kathleen knew the turnoff to Rainbow Trailer Park would be hard to see. It was hard to find even in broad daylight, but Kathleen also knew the canyon well enough after years of driving to Flagstaff that she trusted herself to find it.

In a few minutes, she saw the lights of the trailer park, and turned sharply right, heading for the low-water crossing over Oak Creek, noticing too late the barricades, hitting them. She braked hard but found the car moving despite her efforts, and realized in surprise she was surrounded by water; the force shoving her car down the raging creek.

She screamed, turning the wheel in a fruitless effort to make the vehicle behave. She felt the icy hand of the river as it pushed water into the open window. Instinctively, she knew the window was her only chance for deliverance from the raging water.

The water flung its new toy sideways—with the driver's side lodged against two huge sycamores growing in the middle of the creek. The car hung there giving Kathleen time to shove herself out the open window. She grabbed onto a low branch, trying to move her body away from the car, knowing the rising water—racing now at flood level—would soon propel it out into the open creek, taking her with it. She found a higher branch and clambered up into a niche in the tree, water swirling all around her in the blackness. As she did, she felt a searing pain in her left side, as if a sword had been thrust into her by some unknown hand.

The surging water rose in a roar, and she could hear the screaming of her car's metal against the trees, digging in, trying to save itself from the torrent, but the creek was rising too fast, and the car groaned as it was thrown into the main channel—the sycamores shuddering as they let go of their burden.

She clung ferociously to the tree for what seemed like an eternity, freezing water swirling around her legs. She touched her side feeling the deep wound, wondering what could have caused it, questioning vaguely if she and her precious child would survive the night. Once when she was lucid during the long, cold hours, she cried out for Richard to help her, but there was only the roar of the creek.

As night moved into the early morning hours, the anguish from her wound woke Kathleen from a period of semi-consciousness. It was worse than any pain she had ever felt, and she considered letting go of the tree, knowing the deep waters would quickly end her agony.

As her energy to hang on grew weaker, and the sound of Oak Creek called to her, she began to wonder about the value of her life without Richard. Yet, even though her mind was fuzzy with pain, Kathleen began repeating the words of Father O'Malley: Perhaps she had loved unwisely, but she had loved. And yes, she had to hold on because of the wondrous gift God had given her.

As the light of dawn peaked through the clouds, a thought came to her: "Maybe love is all God wants," she said, half aloud, clinging tighter to the tree, suddenly determined to survive, determined to love again.

Christmas morning appeared bright and cold, and with it, the level of Oak Creek began dropping. Kathleen heard voices and suddenly felt herself being lifted by strong hands. As she was carried to an ambulance by a search and rescue crew, she heard the declarations of old John Perkins and smiled despite her pain.

"It's a miracle, Kathleen, a miracle," he yelled above the roar of Oak Creek.

"I thank God on this Christmas morn that you're alive! Don't you worry girl...we've still got time to get the bastards!"

ABOUT THE AUTHOR

Geraldine Birch has lived for many years in or near Sedona, Arizona, where this novel takes place. A national award winning columnist for the *Sedona Red Rock News*, Geraldine intimately knows Sedona—-her various positions have included that of newspaper reporter, public information officer for the City of Sedona, and Assistant to the City Manager for Arts and Culture.

Also by Geraldine Birch

<u>The Swastika Tattoo</u>

<u>Vision of a Happy Life</u>
<u>A Memoir</u>

I hope you have enjoyed *Sedona: City of Refugees* as much as I have enjoyed writing it. I invite you to connect with me at any of the coordinates below. I look forward to hearing from you.

Webpage: geraldinebirch.com
Twitter: @talesbygerry

DISCUSSION GUIDE

1. What did you like best about this book?

2. What did you like least about this book?

3. If you were making a movie of this book, who would you cast?

4. Share a favorite quote from the book. Why did this quote stand out?

5. What do you think of the book's title? How does it relate to the book's contents? What other title might you choose?

6. Which character in the book would you most like to meet?

7. If you got the chance to ask the author of this book one question, what would it be?

8. What aspects of the author's story could you most relate to?

9. What do you think of the book's cover? How well does it convey what the book is about? If the book has been published with different covers, which one do you like best?

10. Why do you think the author chose to tell this story?

THE SWASTIKA TATTOO

Geraldine Birch

CHAPTER 1

September 1944
Arizona

The question exploded upon Rudolf Meier like a torpedo hitting the hull of a German U-boat.

His head jerked violently to see who could possibly have voiced such an outrage and then Rudolf's gaze landed on the son of the farmer who owned the fields where he and other Nazi prisoners of war labored.

"Why do the German people still believe in Hitler?" the youth asked, unexpectedly throwing his inquiry into the stifling air. In that terrible moment of frozen impotence, Rudolf knew he would never forget the brazen American kid who stood in the midst of a scorching Arizona cotton field, leaning against the wooden handle of a hoe.

The German straightened suddenly from his bent position where he had been digging fiercely at a tenacious weed. "Why do you ask such a thing?" Rudolf spat out his words, rage soaking his voice. Wasn't it bad enough he suffered such degrading work tending the hated *baumwolle*? Rudolf felt no better than a lowly nigger in this parched American wasteland, and now there was the added injury of a stupid American questioning the German people's love for *Der Führer*. Like the small flame of a match to a cigarette, Rudolf's fury lit the crumpled edge of his German soul.

The teenager answered Rudolf's angry words without flinching. "Well, in school yesterday—in my civics class—we were discussing the war and our teacher said the German people would gladly follow Hitler into…well, into Hades. Of course, you need to understand my teacher's brother was killed in the Normandy invasion…fighting you guys, so maybe that's why she thinks that. I heard you speak English to the guard, so I thought I would ask you why the German people still believe in Hitler."

Rudolf stared at the American with unwavering suspicion. He guessed him to be about seventeen. Rudolf's first inclination was to retort he was a prisoner and not allowed to talk to impudent farmers' sons, but he knew the sluggish guards did not care. Deciding to answer the question after a long moment, Rudolf looked around to make sure none of the other POWs could hear; he did not want to be seen talking with the enemy.

"We believe in Adolf Hitler because he made life better for us," Rudolf said, trying to keep a calm demeanor, but his right eye began twitching. "Before Hitler, under the Weimar Republic, there was no work for the German people because of the injustice of the Treaty of Versailles. The *Führer* brought food to our tables, gave us work for our hands. He is our leader, our strength."

The teenager digested that for a moment and then countered, "Yes, but he's led you into this awful war. Germany is losing…"

Rudolf's face, burned brown from the Arizona sun, blanched. He wanted to strike out against this idiot who voiced such blasphemy, but he knew the trouble he would be in if he did. Instead, in a measured tone, he said, "Don't be so sure of that," and then he abruptly turned from the source of his enmity, his eye still twitching against his fierce will. Rudolf quickly found another patch of weeds in an adjacent cotton row to hack into, hoping it would alleviate his wrath.

Moments later when Rudolf glanced back at the farmer's son, he saw a quizzical look, as if the youth wanted to say more, but the guards called the men together to take them back to Camp Papago Park. Rudolf carried his hoe to the shed at the end of the field and turned it in; he was glad for the end of this day and the disrespectful questions by the American.

Back in his barrack, Rudolf removed his boots and placed them carefully at the foot of his cot, and then he stripped off his clothes, filthy with the dust of the cotton field and his sharp-smelling sweat. He dropped them on the floor, one on top of the other in a messy pile, and then sat wearily on his cot in his underwear. The interminable heat was even more stifling in the small barrack, and Rudolf's longing for the green of his beloved homeland permeated his being. Disgusted with his circumstances, Rudolf's thoughts turned easily to the conversation with the American bastard.

He pondered the heresy of the question about German fidelity to Adolf Hitler and then his mind roamed through his knowledge about democracy. Considering it from all angles—what he had been taught in the Third Reich and what he had viewed himself as a prisoner of war—Rudolf determined the American democratic system was a farce. It was beyond logic that every citizen could have a voice in their government, and the turmoil of the failed Weimar Republic imposed upon Germany after WWI certainly proved that.

Rudolf smiled faintly, knowing the German people would never again want self-governance because only *Der Führer* knew what was best for the Fatherland. With all his heart, Rudolf Meier believed in the *Führerprinzip*, the obligation that everyone must obey the nation's leader. Germany's glory was because its leader, Adolf Hitler, had led the country out of its economic crisis, and spread its military force far and wide throughout Europe. While he conceded the *Wehrmacht* was pulling back now on all fronts, that would soon change, and the world would crumple once again under Germany's might. Rudolf felt certain of the Fatherland's triumph, and when that moment happened, America—this country of mixed races and a foolish belief in individual freedom—would simply capitulate.

Although he grudgingly acknowledged the economic strength of America, he believed it to be a country riddled with Jew bankers and bank-robbing Dagos busy lining their own pockets. Rudolf shook his head in wonderment:

Americans had no thought for the national community like Germans—they were too busy stealing from one another other in their capitalistic greed.

This excerpt from *The Swastika Tattoo* can be purchased at your favorite retailer, at amazon.com or smashwords.com.

ACKNOWLEDGEMENTS

To my beloved husband Joe. Without his unfailing encouragement, I could never have written this story.

To my sons for always believing in me.

Made in the USA
Las Vegas, NV
05 February 2023

66969257R00132